SO-CAW-938

IT'S WHAT SHE
Wanted

A Novel

Ronald Goodman

"The safest place in Korea was right behind a platoon of Marines. Lord, how they could fight!"

—MAJOR GENERAL FRANK E. LOWE
US Army; Korea, 26 January 1952

For Pam
Jersey girl working the angles
And on the lookout for strawberries

IT'S WHAT SHE
Wanted

From the Ground Up

Aaron hears something or *someone* walking among the leaves and matted grass near his tent on a rainy night deep in the interior of central Missouri's Lake of the Ozarks. At first he thinks it simply the sound of rain falling softly on the canvass, but it draws closer with the crunch of an acorn, breaking of a twig; too heavy a step for nocturnal critter, he believes. He quietly sits up in his sleeping bag and reaches for a .45 then snaps the clip into place. He is about to pull the tent's flap open to have a look at his visitor when a small, rather plaintive voice, female, speaks: "Hello, anybody home?"

He sticks his head out of the tent's entrance while keeping a hand on the gun. The woman is alone and she moves a step or two closer when seeing Aaron. Though quite small, there is a maturity to her face and Aaron judges her to be in her late 20s or 30s. She is wearing a poncho and her hair, wet and stringing into her face from beneath the hood, is so blonde it looks ghostly. A backpack beneath the poncho gives her the look of a hunchback. Trash bag dangles from one hand. "What's up?" Aaron says.

"I was walking along the shore earlier today and I saw you at the crest of the bluff and going to your tent. I had a tent but it's no good anymore. I don't have a place to get out of the rain. Would you mind sharing your tent with me for tonight? I won't take up much room and I have my own sleeping bag," she says, hoisting the trash bag.

"Hold on, let me light the lantern." When the propane lantern is illuminating the tent's interior, Aaron says, "Come on in." He extracts himself from the sleeping bag, pulls on a pair of cargo shorts then scoots to one side to allow his visitor to enter. A four person tent, more or less, but Aaron has always been its only occupant until now. She pulls the poncho off over her head, throws it to the ground beside the tent then unslings the backpack and sets it and the trash bag near the tent's opening. Aaron retrieves them.

Inside, she releases her breath with a rush, blowing out her cheeks, and says, "Thank you. I didn't know what I was going to do."

"No problem," Aaron says, propping himself up on one elbow. "Do you have a towel for your hair?" he adds.

"Yes, here in my backpack. The wind kept blowing the poncho's hood off my head. I hate those things." She opens the pack and withdraws a towel. Extending a damp, cold hand, small as a doll's, she introduces herself: "I'm Amanda. What's your name?" She notes that the lower half of his left leg is gone, just below the knee.

"Aaron."

"How long have you been camped here?" she says, taking up the towel and beginning to dry her hair. She glances at the leg again and Aaron notes it.

"A while ... I lost part of my leg in Afghanistan."

"I'm sorry," Amanda says, ceasing toweling her hair for the moment.

"So, where are you headed?"

"Nowhere, really; I'm homeless right now—well, for about a year. I got tired of staying in shelters, St. Louis, mostly, and I decided to come to the Ozarks and I ended up on this lake. It's so peaceful and nobody bothers me. The only bad thing is that there's no good place to panhandle. I tried it at Osage Beach but a cop ran me off. My father was in the Army, Vietnam. He was lucky, though. He didn't get hurt or killed."

"I was in the Marines."

"God, I love Marines to *pieces*, the Toys for Tots thing they do at Christmas."

Aaron nods then sits up Indian fashion on top of his sleeping bag.

"Are you homeless or just camping?" Amanda says.

"Not exactly homeless, I guess. I get a disability check. I could go back to work, but I decided to take it easy for a while. I bought this lot. I didn't have enough money to build anything right now so I got a tent. I have an old Suburban parked near a little country church back in the woods a ways. The church isn't used anymore. It sits near a small graveyard. I think it's why I got the lot so cheap, too close to graveyard for most prospective buyers. It doesn't bother me. If it gets really stormy, I head for the church and sleep on a pew and hope that my tent is still here when I come back."

"It's a great tent," Amanda says, looking about at the interior while she towels her hair. "It must be nice to own some land, nobody can kick you out. You know, it's your place and everything. What kind of work did you do before you...?"

"I taught high school, English lit mostly, some science when they needed me to. By the way, have you had anything to eat?"

"Not since morning. Some people on the deck of their lake house saw me coming along the shoreline with backpack, trashbag and everything. They invited me up for breakfast. They were *so nice* and I think they were rich."

"I have a sub sandwich you can have and I'll heat some soup for you, might go down pretty well after being out in the rain."

"Oh, that sounds good."

Aaron rummaged about in a corner of the tent and found a one burner propane stove. He turned to his guest and said, "What kind of soup do you like?"

"Anything."

"Chicken noodle?"

"Great."

He finds the sub sandwich in an ice chest and hands it to her then puts a match to the stove and opens the can of soup.

Gorgeous face, Aaron muses, glancing at the young woman. Though she is missing a lower front tooth, he thinks it detracts little from her natural good looks. Her lips are full and slightly pouting. There is an intelligent look in her dark eyes and she forms her words carefully and with ease. She has an animated way of punctuating her conversation with her left hand, as though it were calling then dismissing her thoughts. Aaron wonders what has brought her to her present state.

Finished toweling her hair, she pulls a hoodie off over her head, unleashing breasts, braless without question, that threaten to rip a worn and faded Mountain Dew tee shirt to shreds. "Good God!" Aaron mumbles.

"What?" Amanda says softly, glancing at Aaron while spreading the damp towel over her backpack.

"Oh, nothing."

With the soup heated Aaron poures it into a bowl and hands it to his quest. "So, tell me everything about yourself that's none of my business," Aaron says, settling back on his sleeping bag and propping himself up on a pillow.

Amanda laughed as she put a spoon to her soup. "I grew up in Des Moines. I have a couple of sisters there, mom and dad, too. They retired from farming a few years ago. I guess I'm the proverbial black sheep of the family. I quit high school in the 10th grade, got into drugs but kicked the habit—with the help of rehab—and I never got back into that crap. But I think that I was such a disappointment to my family they never really forgave me. Anyway, being around them didn't feel like home anymore, so I split—for good."

"How did you end up in Missouri?"

"I stowed away on a Mississippi river barge at Davenport, Iowa. They found me and made me get off at St. Louis. I hung out there for a year but got tired of the shelters and sleeping behind dumpsters. So, here I am. How about you, Aaron?"

"I've got family in Kansas City, mother and father, a couple of brothers. We're cool but don't keep in touch all that well. I graduated from Cornell University and taught high school, as I said. Some of my friends from college went to Afghanistan to fight. I started feeling guilty, like I was letting them do all the dirty work. I took a leave of absence from teaching and joined the Marines. After some training at Quantico, Virginia it didn't take long for them to ship me to Afghanistan. That's where this happened," Aaron said, lifting the leg a bit. "Roadside bomb; I was lucky. The thing didn't go off with quite the force it was meant too, so it only got part of me, some shrapnel wounds here and there but nothing life-threatening The Marines fixed me up with this." He reaches behind him and finds a prosthetic leg. Saving my knee was a blessing. I can walk pretty well."

"Were you married?" Amanda says, spooning her soup.

"Yeah. My wife didn't want me to quit teaching and join the Marines. I guess she got a bit too lonely while I was gone. She met someone else and filed for a divorce. When I came home and she found out that I had lost part of my leg, she wanted to come back to me. But I felt differently about her. She didn't even look the same to me; weird, like she was somebody I never knew. Well, that's enough about me."

"Like I said, I dropped out of school in the 10th grade. But English was my favorite subject. I hated that stupid sentence diagraming, though. It never made any sense to me. I sometimes thought the teacher was lazy and hadn't come to class prepared, so he stuck us up at the blackboard. I've always wanted to be a writer."

"Have you written anything?" Aaron says, stretching across his sleeping bag and fetching a bag of potato chips and offering the bag to Amanda. She declines.

"I wrote a couple of short stories, but never sent them to a publisher."

"Do you still have them?"

"No. I got depressed as hell and pitched them."

"You should have kept them."

"I guess. What are you're plans for tomorrow?" Amanda says.

"I've got a fourteen foot fishing boat tied down below. I have a trotline strung out from the base of the bluff. I'll check it early in the morning."

"What's a trotline? I'm from Iowa."

"It's a line, oh, 80 feet or so, tied to the bank and stretched across a river or out into a lake and anchored on the end with a rock or cement block. They're called throw lines sometimes. We tie jugs at different intervals to hold the line at the depth we want."

"How many fish hooks?" Amanda says, finishing a bite of the sub sandwich and sampling her soup once more.

"About 30, maybe a little more, that's all the state of Missouri will allow per line."

"Mind if I go along?" Amanda says, setting her soup bowl down.

"Not at all. You're starting to look awfully tired," Aaron adds.

"I'm exhausted. A limb fell from a tree where my tent was pitched—fortunately I wasn't in it—and ripped a gigantic hole in the side. I started walking in hopes of finding a cave to stay in, but no luck. That's when I saw you."

"I'm glad you did. And you're safe with me. I'm a gentleman."

"Oh darn—just kidding."

Aaron smiles with tongue in cheek.

Dawn brakes clear and crisp on this late April morning. Song birds have begun their chorus. Grey squirrels, busy with recovering what they burried last fall, are cutting nuts in the tops of tall, scally bark hickory. Aaron is the first to wake. He reaches for his watch: it's *6:30 a.m.* Looking toward Amanda's sleeping bag he sees only a lump. He'll get coffee going then wake her.

He fires up the propane stove then sets the percolator above the flame. He had tried instant coffee when first taking up his abode in the tent, but he quickly grew tired of it. There's nothing like the aroma of *real* coffee brewing and it soon caused the lump in Amanda's sleeping bag to shift. She sticks her head out and smiles. "Good morning," she says.

"Good morning to you. How about a cup of coffee, sausage and eggs?"

"Wow, just like home," she says, pulling herself up in the bag.

With coffee brewed, Amanda nurses a cup while Aaron starts breakfast. "After we check the trotline we'll head on down to Pine Cove Store and get a bag of ice and a few groceries," Aaron says.

"Do you think you caught anything?"

"Fishing isn't the best right now, water's still pretty cold, but we'll see."

The sausage and eggs are done and the two of them sit with plates on their laps. Aaron refreshes their coffee cups. "I hope I'm not a bother to you, Aaron," Amanda says, forking a bite of sausage."

"No bother at all. You're good company."

"Thanks. There's nothing worse than feeling unwelcome. I've been homeless for a while and sometimes I get to feeling like I'm something people are afraid they'll step in and track into their house."

"I've never been homeless, you know, on the street, and I can only imagine what it would be like having no place to call home."

"It's not a good feeling."

"Well, if you're not in a hurry to get somewhere, you can stay as long as you like. It gets a little lonely out here in the woods with just me and the critters."

"How old are you, Aaron?"

"38."

"I'm 32. You're a good looking dude, Aaron. You have the brownest eyes I think I've ever seen."

"Thanks. They are what they are."

With breakfast finished, Aaron sets the dishes aside for now. He finds a couple of coffee mugs. "It'll be cool on the water. We'll take a little coffee along." He finds a sweatshirt and Amanda donned her hoodie. Aaron puts on his prosthetic leg, fetches a spare ice chest then the two of them set out along a path that will lead them to the lakeshore and the boat.

The bow of the old aluminum Starcraft is pulled onto the bank where the limestone bluffs taper down to the water's edge. The boat is chained to a tree and pad-locked. A ten horse Johnson outboard is tilted forward, elevating its prop so that it won't drag on the lake's bot-tom. Aaron unlocks the chain and pushes the boat from the bank. "Hop aboard," he says. Amanda climbes over the gunnels and takes a seat in the bow. "Better put on that," Aaron says, pointing to an orange life jacket.

"Where's one for you?" Amanda says while getting into the life jacket.

"Only got one. I'll pick up another one when we get to the store."

Getting aboard as the boat slowly drifts away from the bank, Aaron moves aft then lets the motor's lower unit into the water and gives the pull cord a yank. The motor belches a faint cloud of blew smoke then begins running smoothly.

Navigating a few yards out from the shore, Aaron points to three plastic milk jugs floating in line 80 feet out into the lake. "That's my line," he says above the hum of the outboard; Amanda smiles and nods.

Nearing the line where it is tied into a washed out ring in the ancient wall of limestone, Aaron shuts the motor down and lets the boat drift easily toward the base of the bluff. Reaching it, he finds the line and be-gins to pull the boat along. The first hook is clean. "Hand me that bucket, would you, Amanda?"

The bucket contains live crawfish, though a couple of them have died and are turning white. Aaron fastens a live one onto the hook then begins to slowly pull the boat along the line once more. Two more hooks are stripped clean.

Nearing the halfway point, Aaron stops and quietly holds the line, rolling his eyes toward Amanda. He eases the line a bit higher out of the water and motions for her to take hold of it. "I feel something jerking," she says.

"I think we've got something out there someplace," Aaron says as he resumes progress along the line.

"What do you think it is?"

"Flathead catfish like live bait. Females are usually laying eggs along shallow shelfs this time of year."

Twenty feet up the line, the water begins to swirl as the catch is being drawn nearer the surface. "Hand me that net, please," Aaron says. "Looks like a bluecat," he adds while carefully lowering the net beneath the thrashing fish. "Nice one, too, five or six pounds, I'd guess."

Amanda claps her hands exictedly. "Wow!" she cries.

With the fish aboard and the rest of the hooks bearing no catch but rebaited, Aaron starts the outboard and heads for Pine Cove Store.

Reaching their destination, Aaron pulls alongside a dock and Amanda jumps out and secures a line. A path runs at an upward angle for twenty yards, crosses a gravel road then ends at the store's front. Aaron opens a screened door with a rusted metal panel advertising Butternut Bread. Seeing the couple enter, an older man in bib overalls arranging candy bars behind the counter salutes and says, "Good morning, Lt." Amanda glances at Aaron upon hearing him called Lt.

"Good morning to you," Aaron says. Approaching

the counter, he introduces Amanda. "Well, we just need a bag of ice, a few groceries and a life jacket."

The two of them stroll among the isles, only 4 of them and confer with each other about what might go good with the catfish for lunch. "Why did he salute and call you Lt?" Amanda whispers.

"I was a 2nd Leutenant in the Marines." Amanda gazes at him as they make their way along the shelving.

Having gathered what they want in grocery items, a life jacket as well, Aaron stops near a shelf containing a few tablets, pensils and pens, envelopes and the like. He picks up 3 rather faded yellow legal pads and blows the dust off of them. He finds a 5 pack of ballpoint pens then turns to Amanda and says, "I think you and I should write a story."

"What could we write about?"

"Oh, we'll think of something ... something fun, not about war. We can set it here on the lake, come up with some fetching characters."

"When should we start?"

"When we get back," Aaron says as they move toward the front of the store and the cash register. "I have an idea about how to get chapter one started, then you can dive in."

"I don't know if I can do it."

"I think you can," Aaron says, falling silent as he finds money in the front pocket of his shorts. "We've got some great hiking trails. We'll walk together and brainstorm. We can cruise the coves, too, stimulate our imagination."

"Let's do it," Amanda says as they leave the store

and head for the boat. "How do we get a bath?" she adds, shifting a paper grocery bag in her arms. Aaron has the life jacket in one hand and a ten pound sack of ice dangling from the other.

"In the lake, weather permitting."

"Lt."

"Yeah."

"Would making love hurt your leg?"

"Probably not ... might be good for it," Aaron says, glancing at his friend. "I guess we'll have to see."

"Yes, we'll just have to see."

Heading the Starcraft back down lake and toward home, they pass a couple of boats. One was a fishing boat and the other an eighteen-foot Mark Twain Stern Drive; occupants in both wave and salute. "Everybody keeps saluting you," Amanda says somewhat encredulously above the hum of the outboard.

"They're very patriotic around here," Aaron says. Amanda only nods and gazes at Aaron for long moments.

Back at the tent, Aaron cleans the fish, wraps it in foil and places it in the ice chest. "We'll fry it for lunch," he says.

The two of them sit on their sleeping bags. Amanda crosses her legs Indian fashion, draws a deep breath and releases it slowly then says, "You got a Purple Heart for getting wounded, didn't you?"

"Yes."

"Could I see it? I've never seen one, you know, in real life."

"Sure." Aaron draws a backpack to him and rummages about in it and finds the Purple Heart. Something else in the same pocket from which the Purple Heart was found glistened for just an instant. Aaron quickly stuffs it back into the pocket then hands Amanda the Purple Heart.

She holds the medal gently, almost reverently. "It's beautiful and crafted so well," she says, turning it this way and that. Handing it back to Aaron she says, "What was that other thing in your bag, the shiny one that you stuffed back into the pocket so quickly?"

"Just something."

"Well then could I see the *just something*?"

Aaron puts the Purple Heart back in the backpack and withdraws a Silver Star with its attached ribbon. He hands it to Amanda. She turns it over in her hands. "I've seen one of these. It's a Silver Star for Valor. My dad showed me a photo of one that his buddy got in Vietnam." Her eyes glistened with moisture. She cleared her throat then said, "This is why everybody is saluting you, isn't it?"

Aaron shrugged his shoulders but says nothing.

"Please tell me what you did to get this."

Aaron blows out his cheeks in resignation then says, "I was on patrol with my platoon. It was just after daylight. I'd had this gut feeling since getting out on the road that this wasn't going to be a good day. It was my third tour and I didn't think it was going to be a charm. Roadside Bombs—IEDs they're sometimes called—had been hell for days."

"What's an IED?" Amanda asked.

"Improvised Exploding Device. They're crude but

affective. Anyway, one of my younger men, Private Harris, was walking a few yards ahead of me. I saw an odd looking rise in the ground and he was heading straight for it. IED screamed in my head. I bolted toward him and yelled, IED, Harris! He turned toward me just as he reached the spot where I thought the bomb was planted. I hit him like a blitzing linebacker. He must have tumbled ten yards."

Amanda laughed as tears rushed to her eyes. She noted how powerfully Aaron's upper body was built.

"The damn thing blew up and took off the lower part of my left leg. I must have been airborne when I hit the guy. That may have saved me from losing both legs, or being killed. Private Harris landed far enough away to escape injury. I got a phone call from his mother while I was in the hospital."

"Tell me what she said."

"She said that every day of her life she lived in fear of seeing Marines coming up the walk and to her door to tell her that her baby had been killed in combat. She broke down on the phone and her husband came on and thanked me for what I had done. Harris' sister came on the phone and thanked me too. Her brother had finished his tour and was home. I talked with him for a few minutes." With that, Aaron drew a deep breath and released it slowly then said, "Let's do some work on our story then we'll cook the fish."

"Yes sir." Amanda snuffed back tears and saluted.

Chapter One

Kenny Decker sat on an outcropping of limestone jutting a half dozen feet above deep water on central Missouri's Lake of the Ozarks. It was a little past dusk and his red and white fishing bobber was getting increasingly difficult to see while floating all too undisturbed a few yards out upon the water's placid surface.

He had been sitting in this spot for an hour with only intermittent trips off the rock to stir his campfire, add a stick or two of wood, and check on a saucepan into which he had deposited a can of chili with beans. Over the years he had tried every brand of canned chili known to man. He always returned to the old standby, Hormel, and sometimes it was on sale for a buck; he'd stock up with a half dozen cans.

Supper straddled two stones near the fire; it only needed to be warmed and kept that way. A camping coffee pot sat next to it; the coffee was brewed and removed just enough from the flames to keep it from boiling further. Kenny had a cup of it in his free hand. He set the cup down for a moment and tightened the fishing line that was sagging onto the surface of the water; not all that crucial, drooping line when using a bobber, he thought, for a tug on the line wasn't what he would be anticipating; dunking bobber would be his clue. If not dunking, then at least a twitch. He had gotten neither.

Changing bait three times saw no improvement. Liver was said to be good for catfish, but it was too easily stripped from the hook by turtles who found the organ particularly tasty; their sharp snout could often rip the liver free without getting hooked, he suspected; a theory. He was a man of many theories, most of which ended up being abandoned. At any rate, turtles were persons of interest if not outright suspects. Minnows and crawfish netted him nothing. A slowly drowning night crawler was presently tempting swimmers down below, presumably; worms carefully threaded on a hook have staying power. Water depth might be a problem, the fisherman considered, especially in early May. Adjusting depth—deeper, shallower—made no difference.

Though Kenny wasn't an *avid* fisherman, he was pretty much a catfish man. Catfish are bottom feeders, most of them, using their whiskers to feel for food along the bottom. Flatheads are an exception; they prefer live bait, pretty much. He doubted that the nightcrawler barely writhing on the hook was all that *live*. He was counting on a fish dropping by that wasn't particularly choosy at the moment. Though he had no idea how deep the water might be, he more or less guessed and split the difference. If there were any fish in the vicinity they apparently hadn't come within a fin's length of the bait; the bobber continued to float sedately.

Behind him, somewhere high in the top of a towering blue spruce whose gently swaying boughs perfumed the air with yuletide scent, seven months early, an owl whooed, as if mocking—or, comforting the fellow below who sat like a frog on a lily pad. It's said that owl hooting is a mating call. Kenny hoped that he wasn't being mistaken for an owl, though he did need a shave.

Not a particularly patient angler, he quit caring if he got any bites or not, so pleasant was this spring evening. And there were no mosquitoes bussing about. A light intermittent breeze was coming across the water from the southwest, scarcely enough to disturb the lake's surface, but lazily carrying what little smoke his fire produced away from him.

Testing his coffee, he found that it had grown lukewarm. He pitched it into the water then laid the fishing rod down and made his way off the rock and onto the shoreline proper. He strode to the back of his new Chevy Tahoe, lifted the hatch and found a glass and filled it half full of ice from an ice chest. Finding a bottle of Jack Daniels, he guessed at an ounce and a half of the whiskey, added water then returned to his fruitless fishing spot.

Kenny Decker was in his mid-forties. He stood a couple inches short of six feet. He was trim, fit, and rather naturally athletic, that is to say he didn't have to work at it all that much. He maintained his weight pretty well at 175 lbs. That's where he felt the best and could tie his shoes easily with a minimum amount of grunting. His hair was dark brown, greying at the temples and thinning on the crown; blue eyes and good teeth though he lost a right side molar which needed pulling a few years back.

A mechanical engineer, he'd had a good job with a firm in Kansas City. Married once, a union that lasted twelve years and produced two children, a boy and a girl—twins, in their early twenties. The girl was something of a vagabond. She was quite artistic. The last her father knew she was working in a Boston bistro and selling her paintings on the sidewalk. Her bistro job was part time and art sales were sporadic. She needed money from dad now and then. The boy, a more practically inclined temperament—not an artistic bone in his jurisprudence body—was in law school at The University of Missouri, Kansas City.

After his divorce, Kenny became intolerably bored with his job as well as the singles wilderness in which he found himself. A little over a decade with the same woman had erased from memory the hard work of trying to find and nurture a relationship. The angst it created wasn't quite worth the hunt, for the time being, anyway, he had decided.

But his life needed a radical change in course. That's when he saw an ad for mechanical engineers to do contract work in Iraq. The war had ended, pretty much, at least in terms of most US combat troops having withdrawn, but it was still a dangerous place; sectarian hate over there made partisan politics in this country look like a quilting party in a church basement, he had concluded. Iraq's infrastructure was in shambles. Off he went, much to the chagrin of his children. He returned two years later with both arms and legs and a bank account in the mid-six digits. He had a condo in Kansas City that he rented out while in Iraq. When he returned home he found that a unit next to his was for sale. He bought it, moved in, and let his renters remain. Investment income, he figured.

Kenny reeled in his fishing line, stripped the deceased, paled out worm from the hook and washed his hands in the lake. He gazed into the top of the great spruce and thought that he could see two eyes looking down at him. The creature was probably disappointed that no fish had been caught and cleaned, leaving behind head and guts.

Returning to his vehicle, he found a bowl, spoon, box of saltines, and took a seat on a log that he had dragged near the fire. Spooning chili from the saucepan into his bowl, he tested it and found it to be plenty warm and quite good. He smacked his lips, looked this way and that and thought that smoke from the fire had added a pleasant, toasty nuance to the flavor: another theory. He took a sip of Jack Daniels and looked out onto the lake that had grown dark with only partial illumination from a nearly full moon that had risen stealthily from the dense timber across the lake, as though that had been the lunar monster's resting place. Somewhere off in the hills he could hear a hound baying on the trail of some poor something or other running for its life, raccoon or fox, perhaps. Should it be a cougar (panther, Ozarkers often called them), the dog would be well advised to lose the scent, Kenny considered while opening the box of crackers. A lightning strike of one of those cat's claws can disembowel a dog with no backup pals or a gun. He once heard a story of a Missouri man being invited to Montana by a friend to hunt cougar. The Missouri man said that he would bring along his three redbone hounds. The Montana friend advised him to leave the dogs at home. The Missouri fellow ignored the advice. When his dogs cornered a cougar in a Montana canyon and rushed to the attack, the big cat killed all three of them.

The fire had burned to a glow of pulsating hickory and oak embers. Kenny added a stick of wood and thought that the modest stoking would do until he retired for the night. He might abuse another worm in the morning, he considered while spooning more chili.

Across the lake he could see only a smattering of lights from cottages, cabins they were usually called in these hills, though many were considerably more than *cabins.* He was camping about midway on this lake that stretched a hundred thirty some miles via its main channel, from Bagnell Dam to the east and Truman Dam on the west. Truman Dam at Warsaw, Missouri was completed in 1979 and backed up the Osage even farther to the west and created Truman Reservoir, usually called Truman Lake. It inundated a little over 55,000 acres. Its counterpart, Lake of the Ozarks, is said to be one of the largest man-made lakes in the United States; a Roosevelt project in the thirties. Bagnell Dam blocked the Osage River and created more shoreline— thirteen hundred miles of it, albeit irregular—than Lake Michigan or the coast of California; some of the coves so large that boaters sometimes become lost, thinking that they are still cruising the main channel.

Kenny finished the chili then refreshed his glass of Old No. 7. Returning to the log by the fire and gazing out onto the rapidly darkening lake once more, he could see a single light moving very slowly upon the water, a boat heading to a favorite fishing spot or retuning home, perhaps. He hoped that their luck had been or would be better than his.

The light on the lake was drawing nearer, having gained no more speed than when he first spotted it, and he could hear the hum of an outboard motor. He thought that the craft might be a hundred yards off, though distance was deceiving in the darkness. Sampling his drink, he figured that his campfire had raised some curiosity, for the boat seemed to have ceased moving and sat dead in the water. He thought now, given the moon's glow, that it was a pontoon with a cabin. After a brief pause, possibly to observe the campfire on the shore, the pontoon continued on down lake.

When searching for a spot to camp in early evening he had more or less wandered about on the gravel and dirt lake roads, peering through dense foliage for the color blue and signs of water. This part of the lake was still relatively remote and hadn't been developed, overly so, at least in the degree in which parts of the lake near Bagnell Dam knew. Though it was nearing dusk, he had seen no more than a half dozen homes—summer or otherwise, among the trees. A shed with open front housed a handful of boats, stored by owners who opted to not transport the boats back and forth from wherever they came from. Upon the side of a hickory near the boat shed was nailed the head of a spoonbill catfish; someone boasting of such a fine catch, though spoonbills are usually snagged. Kenny guessed the fish to have weighed nearly sixty pounds.

Sighting water at last, his next task was finding a way to get to it. He saw nothing that resembled a road leading in that direction. There was an opening in the trees, however, and he thought that he could manage the passage without removing paint and chrome from his Tahoe. He watched for NO TRESPASSING signs and saw none posted. Somebody owned the land, no doubt. He hoped that it was an absentee landlord.

His fire had once more reduced itself to glowing embers. He rose from his seat on the log and washed his dishes in the lake. Kneeling at the water's edge, he heard the soft hum of an outboard motor once more. The pontoon was heading back up lake. The boat was much closer this time. The moon's glow reflected off the hood of a Mercury outboard. Midway in the craft sat a woman at the wheel. He could see her more clearly now. She had quite a mop of hair, blonde—or, strawberry blonde, he fantasized. We do love a redhead, don't we, he thought, sampling his drink thoughtfully. His ex-wife once colored her hair red, which turned out to be rather orange, rendering the witch perennially ready for Halloween.

A small dog was on the lap of the pontoon captain. The dog barked. The woman waved. Kenny waved back. The pontoon had a cabin that occupied half of its deck; a soft amber glow lit its interior. He wondered if the woman was alone. He doubted that the dog was her only companion.

Hearing footsteps behind him, Kenny turned to see somebody coming through the woods with a flashlight. He figured that he was going to get evicted. A large man in bib overalls approached: "Good evening," he said.

"Good evening to you," Kenny returned, standing.

"Carl Jenkins," the man said, extending a hand.

"Kenny Decker. Is this your land?" Kenny said, returning the handshake.

"Yes. I don't mind you fishing here, camp if you like. I just wanted to check and see that I don't have a bunch of druggies." The man had a holstered pistol on his hip.

"No drugs," Kenny said, chuckling.

Jenkins looked out onto the water. The pontoon continued its slow progress up lake. "Josephine and Sodipop," he said.

"Her father?"

"Dog. Cute little outfit, Havanese."

"Interesting name for a dog."

"It likes a saucer of Coke before breakfast, she says. Kind of wakes him up, like coffee does us. Josephine's a real looker. Friendly, God-awful smart ... PhDs in physics and molecular biology—whatever the hell that is."

"Jesus! So, she and the dog just cruise the lake?"

"Experimenting with some sort of new fish bait, she says, something that only attracts catfish."

"What's in it?" Kenny said.

"She won't say."

"Well, whatever it is I could use some. I haven't caught squat."

"If you're around for a while you'll probably run into her. She's up and down the lake 'bout every day, well into the night sometimes. She spends a lot of time on that pontoon but she's got a three-storied log house in a cove up at Gravois Mills; beautiful place, laboratory of some sort on top floor, greenish glow coming from it at night. People joke—not to her face—about her maybe working on another Frankenstein monster or something ... those PhDs she's got. Folks on the lake and back in the hills love her to pieces. She has a big fish fry at her place every summer, usually in the middle of June. Everybody's invited."

"Does she have any family around here?" Kenny asked.

"An older sister in Sedalia; mother and father are dead."

The two men chatted briefly about the weather, how clean the lake was right now, fishing should be getting better when the water warms, then Jenkins made his way back through the woods with his flashlight. Kenny wondered where the man had come from. He had heard no vehicle. The fellow was living nearby, he guessed.

Filling his chili bowl several times with water from the lake, Kenny doused the fire and returned to his Tahoe for the night. He folded down the backseat and unrolled a sleeping bag. He had bacon and eggs in an ice chest. Come morning, he'd build another fire.

Before drifting off to sleep he heard the owl hoot again. Nocturnal creatures, owls; this one was practically on his window sill. He hoped it wouldn't crap on his Tahoe. Hearing an owl hoot three nights in a row is said to be an omen. Michael Martin Murphy heard the owl hoot *six* nights in a row in his song, *Wildfire*. Something—or, someone was overdue.

The faint hum of an outboard; it sounded like Josephine's Merc ... cruising the lake by the light of the moon.

Amanda pulled off her jeans then said, "Your sleeping bag is kind of small for both of us. Maybe we should unzip both of ours all the way, lie on top of one of them then cover ourselves with the other like a quilt."

"Excellent idea."

"I froze my butt off in that lake getting a bath," Amanda said.

"The water will start warming soon," Aaron said, chuckling.

Comfortably naked beneath the covering, Amanda snuggled close to Aaron and said, "I really like the way the first chapter went. Just a first draft, of course, but it shows promise, don't you think?"

"I do," Aaron said while fondling one of Amanda's breasts and feeling the nipple grow errect. "I like what you did with the dog, Sodipop."

"Thanks. At least it isn't spot or tippy." She shifted position a bit to accomadate Aaron sampling the other breast.

"Where did you get the name Josephine and strawberry blonde hair for her?" Aaron said.

"I thought it would be something different, not the usual suave names women get in the romance novels.

And I've always wanted to be a redhead, not this awful cotton stuff I have."

"I love your hair."

"Well, it is what it is," Amanda said. "How's your leg, Lt?"

"Feels good ... so does that."

Amanda giggled then said, "Let's talk about Chapter Two tomorrow."

"Yes, tomorrow."

Chapter Two

Morning broke clear and cool. Kenny reached for his wristwatch lying on the floor of the Tahoe: it was *7:00 a.m.* He was an early riser and sleeping to this relatively late hour was unusual. He began the night with the sleeping bag over him like a quilt, but awakened sometime during the wee hours of the morning, ran the windows all the way up and crawled into the bag.

Getting dressed and passing a hand through his hair while looking into the rearview mirror, he thought that he could use a shave but saw no need for being so fastidious out here in the woods. He would build a fire, put on coffee and get bacon and eggs going. Having used what firewood he collected last night, he scouted about in the timber for kindling, enough to create a small fire for boiling coffee and cooking his breakfast.

The sky was robin egg blue with only a gauzy wisp of clouds whose movement could scarcely be noted. A slight southwest breeze was up and bringing the lake's surface barely to life. Surf that is no surf, not at this early hour and on this lake, was more like water upon a sheet of glass being tilted. It rolled almost imperceptibly to shore, kissed the limestone and smattering of amber gravel then backed away, as though the kiss were stolen. Looks to be a gorgeous day, Kenny thought while placing strips of bacon in a skillet; too nice for just sitting and staring at a bobber and wondering if there is enough wiggle left in a worm to attract any fish out for a bite to eat.

While gathering wood for his fire he had spotted a trail following the shoreline. After breakfast he would douse the fire, lock the Tahoe and see where such a path might lead. So long as he didn't depart from it for any distance, finding his way back to camp should be easy enough. Of course if he wanted to venture from the trail, he could do a Hansel and Gretel and drop a little bread along the way, he supposed, providing birds didn't eat the markers. At any rate, there would be no IEDs or incoming rockets to fear. Copperheads love the Ozarks, but probably too early in the season for many of them to have gotten warm enough to become particularly nasty, Kenny suspected. He put out his fire with water from the lake then found a mug and poured the remainder of coffee from the pot into it. He was in no hurry and had no particular destination. A little coffee along the way would sit pretty well on a morning such as this.

He set out upon the trail that headed in a more or less westerly direction. So narrow was the path that he doubted it had been created by hikers; deer, mostly, maybe an occasional bear. The Ozarks is home to an increasing number of black bear, he had heard. Seeing one in the wild is rare, for they don't interact well with humans, though they have a sweet tooth for donuts. He read that federal legislation had been introduced to outlaw baiting bears. Reprehensible, shooting one of the adorable creatures while enjoying a glazed donut. Though not particularly large, they can weigh as much as 400 pounds, these Ozarks varieties. They are said to be rather reclusive and fairly docile, but an individual was reported to have been attacked and killed somewhere in the Ozarks by a female who thought that her cubs were in danger. No better way to get your ass knocked off than messing with the youngins of a female—two legs or four, Kenny mused while having another sip of coffee.

He had hiked a couple hundred yards or so on relatively level ground, though often having to step over or around tree roots that found their way to the trail's surface. The path began to steepen to about forty-five degrees. He was no more than ten feet from where the terrain dropped rather precipitously sixty feet to the lake below. Pausing and having another taste of coffee, he could see a half dozen boats upon the lake, mostly fishing crafts, he guessed. He saw no sign of Josephine's pontoon. She had probably cruised on back home. Then again, she might have anchored and spent the night in a secluded cove, he imagined; she and Sodipop sleeping in.

The trail began to get more serpentine, due mostly to large protrusions of limestone on the uphill side of the trail that forced intermittent bulges in the path.

Rounding a turn, Kenny saw movement up ahead,

just a reddish flash in the increasingly profuse foliage being beckoned forward by warming, May temperatures. Perhaps a deer, he thought, or a fox squirrel swishing its bushy tail on the trunk of a tree, hoping to detract—the purpose of such tail swishing, it is said—what may be a predator. Senseless warning, tail swishing, Kenny thought; more of an invitation than a distraction. Arrogance, maybe, for few if any critters on the ground were a match for the rodent's speed and agility, though he had once witnessed a tomcat snatch a squirrel from the side of a tree in no more than a single tick of a fine Swiss watch.

The flash of red turned out to be a woman, not a squirrel's tail. She was in full view now. A small dog with a remarkable coat of hair was trotting at her side. The dog barked upon seeing Kenny. Josephine and Sodipop, he guessed. As the two drew near, the dog began switching its curly cue tail. Its master broke into a smile and said, "Good morning."

"Good morning to you," Kenny returned.

"Beautiful day," the woman said, coming to a leisurely stop.

"It is indeed."

"Would you be the camper I saw last night on the shore?"

"It was me."

The woman extended her hand and introduced herself: "Josephine Holland. My dog Sodipop," she added, looking down at the dog. Kenny introduced himself then reached and stroked the dog's head. "We're just out for a little stroll," Josephine said.

"Same here." She's a looker alright, Kenny thought, recalling what his visitor had said last night. Strawberry blonde for sure with what appeared to be more natural curl than a comb or brush could probably manage with any measurable results. Mandatory permanent, compliments of Mother Nature. She was rather tall, leggie beneath khaki cargo pants. Cursive lettering across the front of a white, long sleeved tee shirt read, *Just Say Yes—or, No.* She was shod in hiking boots. Kenny judged her to be in her late thirties or early forties. Her shoulders were broad. Breasts, small, braless, it appeared, though quite bouncy beneath the shirt's cotton, like school children wanting out the door for recess. Typical of redheads, her complexion was fair. A finely chiseled nose hosted a faint cluster of freckles which she hadn't quite matured away from and didn't care to conceal with orange makeup that most redheads require.

Bless their little pumpkin hearts.

Large, almond shaped eyes were hazel. Maria Bartiromo kissin' lips, Kenny mused with tongue in cheek. "Was that your pontoon boat I saw last night?" he said.

"That was us," Josephine said, glancing down at the dog. "Where you from?" she added.

"Kansas City."

"What sort of work do you do?"

"Mechanical engineer."

"Business on the lake?"

"No, just taking some time off, relaxing, do a little fishing."

"Well, it's quieter here at midlake."

Sodipop was getting restless. After a few moments

more of casual talk Josephine excused herself. She and the dog continued on the trail a ways then made a sharp right into the timber and soon disappeared from sight. Her familiarity with the forest needed no well marked trail or bread crumbs, Kenny figured. He sampled his coffee then set out on the course he had set.

The trail began to ascend dramatically for thirty yards. Mounting the crest, Kenny found himself on level ground once more. He guessed that he was now eighty to a hundred feet above the water. He peered off onto the lake and a spectacular view of the main channel meandering lazily to the north. He could see Josephine's pontoon down below, anchored to the shore. She and Sodipop didn't seem to be back aboard yet.

Kenny turned from the lake and continued on the trail which began to swing more inland. He had gone another couple hundred yards when he saw movement up ahead and the bark of a small dog. Josephine and Sodipop, picking up the trail once more and heading back to the pontoon, he guessed. The two of them hadn't noted his approach as he drew nearer. They weren't on the trail at all, he could now see, but in the midst of a small cemetery. The dog was dashing this way and that among the gravestones, numbering no more than a dozen or so. A wrought iron fence with a great deal of vine growing in and out of it encircled the plots. Sodipop saw Kenny first and barked in his direction. Josephine was kneeling and pulling weeds at a gravesite. She looked up then smiled upon recognizing the newcomer. "I've seen you somewhere before," she said, rising to her feet.

"You do look familiar," Kenny said, opening a gate and entering the graveyard. He glanced about the cemetery then settled upon a plot where Josephine had been working. A few crocuses were blooming along the edges of the stones. Weeds had been cleaned from among them and cast to the side. "They don't make them like this anymore," Kenny said. He noted the stones where Josephine had been weeding; none of the names matched hers.

"There's a lot of history here," she said. "Some of the markers date before the Civil War."

"Wow," Kenny said, easing a bit closer. Sodipop was still scouting and sniffing out the grounds, stopping from time to time to see if his tracking was being properly noted.

An old church stood a short distance from the cemetery. Though it was partly concealed by burgeoning spring foliage, it appeared to be the one room variety, often doubling as a school house in days gone by. Its white clapboard siding hadn't seen a paint brush for some time. A steeple was listing just a bit to the north, though it didn't appear to be in any immediate danger of toppling over. The church stood silent watch over the graveyard, a familiar country scene where church and cemetery are often in close proximity; handy for getting casket from church to the place of internment.

"Mom and dad loved the lake," Josephine said. "They would drive in from St. Louis almost every weekend during the summer and spend a couple of week's vacation, too. I practically grew up on this lake. They're both dead now ... not buried here, but they used to

come and do a little mowing, spruce things up a bit."
She reached down for a weed that had been missed. "I
wanted them to have a family plot so that I could come
and take care of their graves like they did for these," she
said, casting about the cemetery.

"Lovely spot," Kenny said, glancing about at the
pristine landscape. Hickory, oak, and wild cherry grew
so dense at times a man would have to keep his hands in
his pockets while walking, he thought. Dogwood, their
buds just beginning to open, were sprinkled among the
greater trees, impervious to the inordinate shade and
crowding; dogwood aren't easily intimidated. "How old
is that church?" Kenny said.

"Pre-Civil War," Josephine said. "But it's had quite
a bit of work done on it over the years when it was used
for worship services. It was closed years ago."

"Kind of peaceful looking, standing there among
the trees," Kenny said, gazing at the rather ancient
house of worship. He thought that he saw a curtain part
just for a moment at a window. "I thought I saw someone at a window," he said, turning to Josephine.

"Yes, that would be Evelyn. She lives there. She and
her husband used to operate a saw mill back in the hills.
He was killed when his logging truck fell on him while
he was underneath working on it. A year after his death,
the house burned. She moved into the church. She has a
son on the west coast, quite a successful lawyer. He
tried to get her to come to LA and live with him and his
family, but she wouldn't budge. So he came back, managed to buy the church and an acre of land that went
with it then had central heat and air installed. The

building is pretty well insulated, believe it or not. Her son had a proper bathroom put in as well."

Not far from the church stood an outhouse, a pro-verbial quarter moon was carved into its door. "The outside needs some paint," Josephine continued, look-ing at the church, "but Evelyn thought it looked kind of rustic as is. Structurally, it's pretty sound."

"How long has she been there?"

"Oh, seven or eight years," Josephine said, pitching another handful of weeds onto a pile. "She used to look after the cemetery, mowing, weeding. She's gotten too old to do much anymore. Her husband is buried here."

"How old is she?" Kenny asked, bending to pull a weed.

"She won't say. But I think she's easily pushing 90. She loves to go blackberry hunting, but had to give it up. I bake a blackberry cobbler now and then and bring it to her."

"Could I meet her sometime?" Kenny said.

"I think that could be arranged. I'm going to come and get her for a fish fry I have every summer. I've got some blackberries frozen that I picked last year. I'll bake a couple of cobblers and send one home with her." Then, "So, how long are you planning to camp?"

"I might stay a week or so, maybe longer, scout more of the trails. I can use the exercise." He stepped to a gravesite near him and plucked a weed and tossed it onto a pile that Josephine had accumulated. He glanced about the cemetery, noting weeds beginning to come on, though not a great many. "I wouldn't mind helping out here some. Beautiful morning for a little weed pulling," he said.

"Be my guest—*their* guest. We'll work as a team if you don't mind."

"Sounds like a plan."

Josephine gathered up the disgarded weeds and strode to the fence and pitched them into the forest. She brushed her hands together and returned to where Kenny had begun to busy himself. "Are you married, Kenny?" she said then looking to see if Sodipop was still within the graveyard's confines. The dog was digging at a hole he had found.

"Divorced, quite a while back."

"Children?"

"A boy and girl, in their 20s," Kenny said. "Daughter lives in Boston; son's in law school, Kansas City. How about you?"

"I never got around to anything long term, too busy with graduate work."

"Carl Jenkins said you have PhDs in physics and molecular biology," Kenny said, straightening and slinging a handful of weeds onto another pile that his partner had begun.

"I do. Not exactly related," she said then looking toward Sodipop once more. "He'll be filthy with that digging. Like most dogs, he doesn't like baths. He's very intelligent, but it obviously hasn't occurred to him that digging means a bath. Havanese breed don't shed, thank God, even with all that hair."

"Fabulous coat. It's in their DNA, digging, I think," Kenny said.

"If there's a cocklebur or sweetgum ball within 10

feet of him, he attracts it like a magnet. I give him a haircut in early summer."

"He's pretty good about not running off," Kenny said, noting that he hadn't closed the gate.

"He could clear that fence with ease. Havanese originated in Cuba. Havana society women love them as lap dogs, soft as a ball of cotton. They're very affectionate; popular in circus acts over there, too, agile and quick to learn tricks."

"He likes a saucer of Coke in the morning, Jenkins said."

"Yes. I don't know if it's very good for him, but he won't eat his breakfast until he has his Coke. I just give him a splash or two. He kept begging for some of mine once when he was just a pup. I dipped my finger into the glass and gave him a taste. I guess he got hooked, the little addict. So I named him Sodipop. My grandfather used to call soda, *sodipop*."

"He'd make a good Coke commercial," Kenny said.

"He would at that," Josephine said, laughing. Then, "I've got a place up at Gravois Mills. If you're going to be around for a while, I'd like to have you for lunch. I'll pick you up with my pontoon."

"I'd like that."

"I think your camp will be okay while you're gone. Carl Jenkins keeps a pretty good eye on things. What do you like to eat?"

"I eat anything I can get in my mouth, so long as it doesn't have anchovies."

"Hold the anchovies," Josephine said. The two volunteer caretakers worked for an hour more then bid each other goodbye for now. They exchanged cell phone numbers. Josephine would call in a day or so.

"I think we might get a pretty good romance going between Kenny and Josephine," Amanda said as she and Aaron walked arm-in-arm along a trail just south of the old church."

"I think so," Aaron said. "You've got a good feel for that part of the story."

"I'm curious about what you plan to do with her PhDs, a little deep for me," Amanda said.

"I've got something fun in mind, if I can pull it off."

"You pulled it off last night, baby," Amanda said, bumping Aaron's hip. "How's the leg?"

"I hardly know part of it is gone."

"My treatment must have worked." The trail looped back toward the church and graveyard. When it came into view Amanda said, "I love those old graveyards. I want to be burried in one, if I don't opt for cremation, as so many are these days."

"Saves real estate," Aaron said.

"So, what's up for chapter three?"

"I've got an idea or two."

"Me too," Amanda said. "I think we might be getting on the same page with this story."

"We're starting to click. And the fun is only started," Aaron said. "By the way, how did you come up with that dog? I never heard of one of them, Havanese."

"A neighbor in Des Moines had one. It was the

smartest dog I ever saw. Pricy, though, she paid $2,000 for it, partly because of its coloring, mottled in brown and charcoal, said to up their value."

"Did that dog like a little Coke for Breakfast?" Aaron said, chuckling.

"I doubt it. I just thought Sodipop would be a cute name for a dog, especially with its *addiction*. When I was homeless in St. Louis I used to go to this one McDonald's about every morning. It was amazing how many people came in that early and got nothing but a soda then hurried on to work."

"Regular health nuts," Kenny said.

"After lunch let's start on chapter three—Lt…"

"Yeah…"

"I'm going to pay you back someday, you know, for feeding me and everything."

"Don't worry about it."

Chapter Three

A thunderstorm moved through during the night, bringing with it high winds and hail. Lightning lit the sky like ground zero on the 4th of July. Lying in his sleeping bag while strong gusts rocked the Tahoe, Kenny was glad that he hadn't opted for a tent; it would probably be in the lake by now, him with it, possibly. He wondered if the owl had held its own in the top of the blue spruce. Perhaps better shelter had been found for riding out the storm. If not, it would be missing a few feathers come morning, blown away like dandelion seeds.

Short of being in a tornado's path, Kenny had no fear of storms. Good sleeping weather, he thought, especially on such a night as this while listening to rain pelting the Tahoe's roof. The intermittent rattling of hail, pea sized, he thought, with its fall being broken by dense timber, probably wouldn't damage his vehicle. Frozen golfballs would be a different matter and might coldcock the owl as well. He found that he was growing fond of the creature. He would hate to find that it hadn't survived the night. He hoped, too, that Josephine and Sodipop weren't navigating the lake when the storm hit. He wondered if the craft had a lightning rod. Chances are, though, her degree in physics had persuaded her to cruise on back home well ahead of the storm. This kind of energy she would understand.

Dawn arrived on the lake with a promise of clear skies. Kenny crawled out of his sleeping bag and began getting dressed. Peering out of the Tahoe's rear window while he pulled on a sweatshirt, he cast about to see if the owl was lying beneath the spruce with its feet turned up. He saw nothing of it; a good sign providing the bird hadn't been blown into the lake and gobbled up by something hungry for bait other than what he himself had used.

Dressed and emerging into the cool morning air, Kenny figured that finding dry wood for a fire was hopeless. He'd settle for peanut butter and jelly for now. Coffee would have to wait ... maybe not, for when hearing the hum of an outboard, he turned and saw Josephine's pontoon coming out of a cove and headed his way. He strode to the water's edge, splashed some water into his face to wash sleep from his eyes and ran a comb through his hair. He stood on the shore and awaited the visitor.

"Good morning!" Josephine called, waving when drawing within a hundred feet. Sodipop jumped onto a storage compartment and barked. Kenny waved back and thrust his hands into the front pockets of his jeans.

Josephine cut the Merc's engine and the pontoon eased into the bank. She went forward and threw out a bowline. Kenny gave the hemp a couple turns around a cottonwood. "Quite a storm," she said.

"I'll say."

"Didn't blow you into the lake, I see." She and So-dipop disembarked.

"Did you make it back home ahead of the storm?" Kenny said, bending and rubbing the dog's head.

"We spent the night in a cove that sheltered us a bit from the wind, put down a couple anchors in shallow water, so we didn't get knocked around too much." Then, "I doubt that you've had breakfast."

"None, figured I'd be out of luck with finding any dry wood. I was going to settle for peanut butter and jelly."

"I can beat that. Come on aboard, I'll fix us something. I've got coffee on now."

"I could use a cup," Kenny said, following Josephine and Sodipop onto the pontoon and into its cabin. He sat down on a plush window seat and Sodipop hopped beside him. Josephine fetched cups and poured coffee for the two of them. A bag of Starbucks French Roast beans sat next to a grinder.

"Cream or sugar?"

"Black." Taking the cup from her he sampled the brew; black as wet tar. He thought the stuff could walk up a mountain with Folgers' Juan Valdez and his burro.

"How is it?"

"Excellent. I could use a little hair growth."

Josephine laughed, had a sip from her own cup then set it down and turned to a small refrigerator where she found eggs, sausage, and canned biscuits. She snagged a 16 oz bottle of Coke sitting on the counter and poured a

splash into a saucer and placed it on the floor for Sodipop. The dog hopped to the floor and began lapping the
soda.

"Carl Jenkins, the man who owns the land I'm
camped on says you're experimenting with new fish
bait, something that only attracts catfish. How's it coming along?" Kenny said, turning his coffee cup clockwise
on the counter.

"So so," Josephine said, popping the canned biscuits on the corner of the counter. The cardboard container split open and biscuit dough bulged. She peeled
them out one by one and placed them on a stick free
cookie sheet. "Catfish bait is nothing new, lots of it on
the market," she continued, "everything from stink bait
to artificial worms and crawfish. Mom and dad always
wanted to catch catfish. If they were still around they
would be putting out limb lines where flathead are laying eggs along rocky shelves of the shoreline this time of
year. They would use goldfish for bait ... not allowed
anymore, member of the carp family that conservation
people don't want proliferating in the lake. I'm just trying to develop something with better results that can't
be stripped from the hook."

"Interesting concept," Kenny said, sampling his
coffee. "Are you going to try and market it at some
point?"

"No, just having some fun, keeping bordom at bay."

Kenny had a sense that money wasn't an issue with
this woman. Graduate work is expensive, especially in
pursuit of two PhDs. He doubted that her doctorates
had made her rich, especially given her relative youth.

He didn't know what her late father had done for a living, but a sizable inheritance may have left his two daughters well heeled. "What sort of engredients are you using in the bait, if you don't mind me asking?" Kenny said.

"Trade secret," Josephine said while cracking eggs and depositing them into a skillet. "Are you into particle physics?" she said.

"Probably not," Kenny said, chuckling. "I do find it intriguing, though, just a tad deep for me. The discovery of the Higgs boson particle was pretty much all over the media for a while, practically a household word. Most of us have no clue as to what it is."

"Unique little gizmo," Josephine said. "It has zero spin. It's a gauge of how particles acquire mass. Some have called it the God particle, much to the chagrin of most scientists. Its discovery after having been predicted some years ago created a lot of excitement in particle physics. When the Large Hadron Collider—a much more powerful version—near Geneva, Switzerland cranks up again this year, we might find something else in the debris. That's the hope, anyway."

"Like what?" Kenny said as Josephine set his plate of food on the counter in front of him.

She poured dried dog food into Sodipop's dish and topped it off with a pattie of sausage that she tore into pieces. She fetched her own plate of food and took a seat across from Kenny. "We're in search of supersymmetry," Josephine continued. "That would unify the universe, maybe."

"You've lost me."

"You're not alone," Then, "So, you're a mechanical engineer?"

"Yes."

"What do mechanical engineers do?"

"You name it," Kenny said, forking into his eggs. "It's the broadest field of engineering." After a bite of his egg and sausage, he said, "I recently returned from a two year tour in Iraq—not in uniform—but as an engineer. As you might imagine, their infrastructure is in shabbles."

"Dangerous place," Josephine said, lifting her coffee cup to her lips.

"It paid well. I came back with both arms and legs, more than I can say for a lot of our military."

The two ate in silence for a time then Josephine said, "If you've got no plans for today, I'd like to take you up to Gravois Mills. I've got a 20 pound channelcat we can cook for lunch ... maybe a margarita or two on the deck. I'll bring you back, I swear."

"I'm in," Kenny said, thinking that so long as his Tahoe was safe, he didn't care how long this strawberry headed bombshell kept him.

A light southwest breeze was up when Josephine backed the pontoon away from the bank and set out upstream for Gravois Mills. The big Black Max Mercury outboard purred like a contented cat while the boat's pontoons plied their way through a moderate chop. Sodipop sat on the captain's lap and peered ahead as though he were a necessary compliment to the navigation; first mate. Kenny sat on a swivel seat across from the captain. She had refreshed their coffee cups before getting underway and Kenny nursed his. Sodipop, pink tongue lolling, looked over at the passenger from time to time as if to see if the cruise was being enjoyed. Kenny smiled at the dog and it switched its curly cue tail then returned its attention to the course ahead.

The lake's shoreline was remarkable in its varied landscape. Terrain to the northeast, viewed from the pontoon's present position upon the water, was rather flat, sometimes hosting what looked like swamp grass. A blue heron rose from its midst and took flight. Josephine pointed to it and Kenny nodded. "Beautiful bird," he said above the outboard's hum. Sodipop noted the bird and barked once.

Gazing off the port side of the pontoon, the shoreline often rose rather steeply into dense timber. Limestone bluffs, rising a hundred feet or more at times, stood like towering monuments to the past when this valley hosted only a serpentine river before Bagnell Dam put it everlastingly out of its banks. The river valley was once home to Osage Indians. Kenny could imagine smoke signals wafting away from the bluff's highest points and squaws beating clothes with rocks while doing the family's laundry down below.

"Pine Cove Store over there," Josephine said, pointing toward the western shore."

The main channel began swinging to the north and the first buildings of Gravois Mills came into view. A number of boat docks jutted into the lake. A boy was sitting on the edge of one while his feet dangled into the water. A fishing rod was in his hands and he waved at the pontoon as Josephine began turning into the cove where her lake house stood. Kenny supposed that her boat was a familiar sight to the boy.

Lots along the shoreline were rather large it would appear, for homes—cottages, cabins, perhaps one might say—were not crowding one another. Up ahead Kenny saw what he guessed was Josephine's place, quite impossing, rising to its three stories and well above any other structures nearby. While the pontoon drew nearer, she pointed in the direction of her home. Kenny smiled and nodded in acknowledgment. He noted that the cedar logs had been allowed to weather naturally, a nicely nuanced blending into the forest's close perimeter.

The home's owner was obviously one who liked plenty of natural light, for there was a great deal of glass, double glazed, Kenny figured, to insure insulation as well as strength against storms that could pummel the lake with a vengeance. A half moon deck fronted the first level. Smaller decks, more like balgonies, adorned the second and third levels. A native stone chimney rose from cedar shake roof. Though Kenny had yet to see the home's interior, he guessed that the place would easily push five or six hundred grand these days and that not including the lot upon which it sat. A modest boat dock, fire hose rimming its edges to protect whatever crafts might be moored, obviously belonged to the property. Josephine headed the pontoon in its direction. Sodipop barked and hopped onto a storage compartment and looked toward home.

Bringing the pontoon alongside the dock, Kenny jumped out and secured a line fore and aft. Josephine cut the outboard. "Here we are."

"Beautiful place," Kenny said, surveying the property at much closer range.

"Thank you."

Josephine slung a backpack over one shoulder and, with Sodipop in tow, the threesome made their way along the dock's gangplank and onto a shoreline of fine gravel that ended in thinly growing clover that made up the home's front lawn, gently sloping for 60 feet toward the lake. Kenny suspected that the clover was sewed intentionally for the purpose of not requiring particularly rich soil or frequent mowing.

Reaching a short flight of cedar stairs, Sodipop bounded up them and onto the home's deck. Abundant outdoor furniture was placed here and there. A large, stainless steel grill sat to one side. Kenny and Josephine followed the dog and made their way to a sliding glass door which the owner unlocked with a key. She pushed the glass to one side and invited her guest to enter first. Inside, he cast about the sprawling and tastefully furnished living room. Flooring was of four inch white oak with walnut pegs. A few small and judiciously placed area rugs of oriental design added color to the flooring which dominated the room. Most of the furniture for seating was crushed leather, appropriate for lake houses should someone with a wet bathing suit plop down.

The room's ceiling hosted exposed beams and the roof's cedar decking was visable. Studio lights were mounted upon the beams. A half dozen impressionist paintings hung upon walls, most of which were wood paneling with the exception of a native stone fireplace that ran six feet along one wall. The open kitchen was papered in yellow and burgundy penstripe. An L-shaped bar and six stools occupied one corner of the room. Appliances were copper and blended nicely with the woodsy atmosphere. "Would you like to see my laboratory?" Josephine said.

"I would."

The two of them, with Sodipop close behind, began mounting a flight of stairs situated midway in the livingroom, rising steeply and ascending ten or twelve feet to the home's second floor where generous landing of pine planking led off right and left. A spoked railing furnished protection from falling to the ground floor. Three doorways were along a wall papered in wildlife scenes, most notably a bear and her cub standing in a stream and watching for fish, one of which was firmly in the mother's right claw. "There are two bedrooms, a bath and den up here," Josephine said, pointing to the doors. "My lab is on the top floor," she added while ushering her guest down the landing to a spiraling staircase that led to the laboratory.

Reaching the third floor, Josephine pushed a folding door to one side that admitted her and Kenny into the room. Sodipop bounded in first. The ceiling was vaulted and a sizable skylight shed generous light into the room this time of day. More studio lights hung from cedar beams. The floor was carpeted in plush tangerine, wool that showed little or no wear.

A counter ran along one wall for ten feet then made a sharp right turn into the middle of the room. Suspended above the counter was a forty-two inch flat-screen. An assortment of viles and beakers were ranged neatly along the counter. "What's that?" Kenny said, nodding toward a box about the size of a large microwave oven. Its cabinet was of heavy glass.

"That's Lazarus, my miniature particle detector," Josephine said.

"Finding any?" Kenny said, easing up to the counter and peering through the machine's glass.

"A few. A toy pretty much. I doubt that Geneva's LHC is in any danger of being upstaged," she said, laughing.

"So, what do you do with all those beakers of chemicals?" Kenny said, thrusting his hands into the front pockets of his jeans and gazing along the counter.

"They're mostly for extracting DNA."

"Crime lab?"

"No, just experimenting with an idea or two."

"And what might that be?" Kenny said, increasingly intrigued by the room.

"Another trade secret."

A woman of many secrets, Kenny thought, easing closer to the viles and noting the varied coloring of the liquids.

"Let's go back downstairs," Josephine said. "I'll get the fish ready and we'll grill it afterwhile. How about another cup of coffee?" she added as they made their way to the staircase.

"Sounds good."

Back on the home's main floor, Kenny took a seat at a counter in the kitchen while his host ground beans and put on a pot of coffee. "Does anybody ever call you

Jo, for short?" he said.

"Some relatives and friends tried to stick me with it when I was younger ... compulsive shorteners, our society. But I wouldn't let them. Josephine is a namesake, great grandmother and she always went by Josephine. Kind of old fashioned, I guess, but I insisted on it out of respect for her, though I never met her, of course."

"Was she a redhead?"

"She was," Josephine said, turning and smiling. She strode to a pantry and fetched coffeecake. "A little something with our coffee," she said, finding saucers in a cupboard.

Kenny very much wanted to persue the contents of the laboratory, the green glow in particular, said to be coming from the lab at night, but figured he'd been nosy enough for now. He supposed the glow was coming from the partical detector ... *Lazarus*, interesting name. This woman was up to something—*on* to something, perhaps. He saw no operating table with leather straps in the lab, so he doubted that she was attempting to create another Frankenstein monster. "What sort of work did your father do, if you don't mind me asking?" Kenny said when coffee and cake was served.

"He had a number of Mercury outboard dealerships around the midwest," Josephine said, taking a seat on a stool across from Kenny. "When he died rather suddenly of a massive heart attack, mom sold them and the estate handled the rest."

That explains this woman's relative leisure, Kenny thought, putting a fork to the cake. "Did you teach at a university?"

"I did an associate thing at The University of Miami for a while. I decided that I wasn't cut out for academia. So when I came back for dad's funeral, I stayed on the lake and built this house. It's much larger than what I need, but I was tired of apartments. I love all the room, so does Sodipop."

"Gorgeous place," Kenny said, taking up his coffee cup. "I'd say it's a bit more than a lake house."

"Yes, a bit," Josephine said, rising to get the pot to refresh their coffee. "Some of my neighbors thought that I was outclassing things around here."

"A little," Kenny said, smiling.

"They're good neighbors, though, and most of them aren't here year-round like me. How long to do you think you'll stay at your camp, Kenny?" she said, sampling her own cake and tossing a piece to Sodipop who was patiently waiting.

"I might hang around a couple of weeks or so. Nothing urgent that needs me back in Kansas City."

"It's a pleasant time of year here," Josephine said, "not so hot and mosquitoes aren't out yet, many of them anyway." Then, "I think I'll blacken the catfish for grilling. I've got some potato salad and baked beans … margaritas?"

"I'm in," Kenny said, though he couldn't quite get his mechanical engineer mind off the particle gizmo up in the lab. He was no physicist and aside from reading *Scientific American* once in a while, he scarcely knew quarks and protons from coffeecake crumbs on his saucer.

"Where did you come up with that particle detector idea?" Amanda said while adding a stick of firewood to a campfire just outside the tent.

"When I was teaching science to high school seniors they were particularly interested in the subject," Aaron said, gazing at the sparks that went into the night sky when Amanda put on more wood. "We actually built a miniature detector. But we never could tell if we had captured any particles. But it was great fun. And the kids imagined that we might be breaking new ground in particle physics." Aaron chuckled and said, "That fire feels pretty good tonight."

"It does," Amanda said, taking a seat on a log next to Aaron. "Nights are cool still."

"I've got a bottle of Jack Daniels in one of my duffels," Aaron said. "That should warm us up even more."

"I like a little Coke with mine, Lt," Amanda said.

"You and Sodipop," Aaron said, smiling. "I'll fix you up. By the way," Aaron said, getting up from the log where he was sitting, "did Josephine really need a lake house that big? It's practically a lodge."

"I've always dreamed of having a *big* house with tons of room. Having one like hers on the shores of a lake would be really cool."

"Well, you can at least fantasize and pretend that it's your house," Aaron said turning to go. He felt a curious sense of guilt at having nothing more to offer his friend than a tent.

He returned shortly with two glasses tinkling with

ice in the amber whisky. He handed Amanda a can of Coke and she poured a little of it into her glass. She took a sip from the contents then said, "So, now that you've got me boxed into a corner with that detector—*Lazarus*—what do you have in mind for my brilliant character, Josephine, to do with it?"

"She's your character, baby," Aaron said, smiling and sampling his drink.

"Thanks a lot, Lt. I'll need some hints you know. I'm no scientist."

"Neither am I," Aaron said. "But I've got an idea I'll pitch to you at the proper time."

"How *generous* of you," Amanda said, swirling the ice in her glass. "I'll need a little more than Jack Daniels for getting any sleep tonight."

"That can be arranged."

Chapter Four

Kenny spent the next couple of days relaxing at his camp. Fishing luck emproved: he reeled in a half-dozen crappie the size of his hand and a channelcat, nothing close to what Josephine had grilled. Over margaritas they talked of everything from why three out of five American marriages fail; the known universe continues to expand at breakneck speed; and why shopping carts cause transient autism in adults, especially women. They had no easy answers. The blackened fish was good. And margaritas seemed perfectly suited for such brainstorming while watching an occasional boat ply the waters off the timbered shoreline of Gravois Mills.

Though they exchanged cell phone numbers, neither had called the other since their date. But Kenny sensed that they would be seeing more of each other. He thought once, during the wee hours of the morning, that he heard the hum of Josephine's Merc.

On the third day he got a call from her just before noon. She wondered how he was doing. Good, he said, and fishing was better. She asked if he might want to camp on her side of the lake. There was a spot not far from her, a nice grove of trees near the water. She knew the owners—folks from Wichita—and they wouldn't mind if he camped there. Kenny liked the idea and she gave him directions for Hurricane Deck Bridge that would get him across the lake and near Gravois Mills. She would meet him at the north end of the bridge and escort him to the new campsite.

Breaking camp was simple enough: bury the fire pit and say goodbye to the owl atop his blue spruce home, should the creature be there and it was. Kenny consulted notes he had taken regarding directions, eased the Tahoe back through the woods and onto the road then set out in an easterly direction. He got on his cell phone and called Josephine to tell her that he was on his way. Fortunately, the lake road that brought him to his camp was a main artery, of sorts, and after traveling for what he judged was three miles or so, Hurricane Deck Bridge came into view. A royal blue BMW sat along a shoulder near the opposite end of the bridge. Kenny guessed that it was Josephine, though he hadn't seen what she drove. He suspected that she spent more time on the pontoon than in the car.

Exiting the bridge, Kenny saw the car's driver side window go down. Josephine waved to him. He pulled alongside of her and she said, "Follow me, it's not far."

"Lead the way, lady."

It was a short drive to the proposed camping spot. Kenny's guide parked her car beside a drapping willow. He parked behind her and the two met at the rear of her car. "What do you think?" she said, stuffing her hands into the front pockets of cutoffs and shooting a look at Sodipop who was dashing up and down the beach.

"I like it, nice and close to the water."

"You can see my place through those trees," Josephine said. She pointed in the direction of a stand of red cedar. Part of the roof of her home was visable, perhaps fifty yards away, Kenny guessed. "By the way, I've got a tent you can use," she added. "You'll feel like a real camper."

"I'll take you up on that."

"I'd like for you to come for supper," Josephine said. "I'll grill some ribs."

"Mind if I use your shower? I may be getting a little ripe."

"Be my guest."

Kenny found a change of clothes, gathered some toiletries and set out along the beach. The house was in fact no more than fifty yards away. As he approched, Sodipop announced the visitor's arrival. Josephine was on the deck and setting a covered dish near the grill. She had a bottle of Corona beer in one hand. "Hello," she said as Kenny mounted steps to the deck.

"Which way to the shower?" Kenny said, bending to tousle Sodipop's ears.

"This way, I'll show you." She led her guest into the house and directed him to her master bedroom and a walk-in shower. "I put out a towel and washcloth for you," she said, turning to go.

After shaving and showering, Kenny got into denim shorts and pulled on an   Adidas tee shirt. Returning to the deck, his host found him a bottle of beer from an ice chest. "This should sit pretty well after your shower," she said.

"It will." He took the beer from her and put the cold bottle to his lips.

Josephine began putting ribs on the grill. She closed the hood then sat down beside her guest. She crossed shapely legs and sampled her beer. She was wearing flip flops. Her toenails were painted lipstick red, Kenny noted. "So, how are things going with Lazarus?"

"I"ve been fiddling with the detector's energy level."

"Nothing like a little fine-tuning," Kenny said.

"I had this crazy idea of using the detector to try and get the darn bait to stick together. It kept coming apart as soon as it got in water, which won't do, of course. I've tried oils, even molases—all kinds of stuff— but nothing worked."

"I used to mix Wheaties and Strongheart canned dogfood," Kenny said. "The oil in the dogfood kept the bait together a *little* longer."

"What did you catch?"

"Bullheads mostly, in a small pond near where we lived when I was growing up on the southeast side of Kansas City."

"Finally, I thought, as a last resort, what if I put the stuff in the detector?"

"What happened?"

"Well, when I shut the detector down and opened the door, there were these two nice little cubes sitting so cute side by side. I was afraid to touch them. I put on surgical gloves and gave them a feel. They were just warm, and soft, kind of like sponges. I tried to pull one of them apart but it just went back into its neat shape about the size of an ice cube."

"That's the bait?" Kenny said.

"Yes. I couldn't get a hook into the stuff, so I tied one of them on the end of a fishing line. I cast it into the lake, right out there off the end of my dock. No bites. I was going to give it up as a dumb idea when it occurred to me that maybe I could add a little bit of stuff I mixed in one of those viles you saw in my lab."

"What was the stuff?" Kenny said, sampling his beer and gazing at his guest off the side of his face. She didn't answer. Another secret, he thought.

"I did just that and cast the bait back into the lake. It had no sooner hit the water when the 20 pound channelcat I grilled a few days ago grabbed it and wouldn't let go."

"Wow," Kenny said, taking another drink of beer.

"It took me a while to reel the thing in. Sodipop was going bananas."

"Have you tried it again?" Kenny said.

"No." She got up and turned the ribs.

After twenty minutes more of casual conversation, Josephine found that the ribs were done and said, "It's a pleasant evening—too cool for many flies—let's eat out here." Kenny followed her into the house where they found eating utensiles and added potato salad and cole slaw to plates before returning to the deck for ribs.

While they were eating, Kenny said, "What do you think happened inside that gizmo you've got up there?"

He nodded toward the third floor of her house and the lab.

"I'm a phycists so I do have a theory. Every theory must make a prediction, however. If the prediction doesn't come to pass, the theory must be abandoned."

"Spoken like a true scientist," Kenny said, laying a rib down in his plate and wiping his hands on a napkin before having a drink of beer. Then, "Let's hear the theory."

"I think that my mini detector stumbled onto a sub-atomic particle similar to the Higgs boson. I saw something unusual, with zero spin, like the Higgs. The Higgs boson has the capacity to draw matter into a mass. It's believed that most of the universe is made up of dark matter and dark energy. We can't see them because they don't have photons for emiting light. But we think it exists because there aren't enough visible bodies in the universe to account for the amount of gravity needed to keep them all in orbit and from flying apart."

"You've lost me," Kenny said.

"You're not alone," Josephine said, chuckling. "My theory is that a particle mimicking the Higgs has found its way into my detector and created the cubes."

"Anything like this ever happened before that you know of?" Kenny said.

"Not to my knowledge. Some cosmologist—evangelical types—think that the universe has a sense of humor," Josephine said, chuckling and having another drink of her beer.

"What do *you* think?"

Josephine shrugged her shoulders. Then, "We're

learning something new all the time about the cosmos. Humor isn't out of the equation, in my opinion."

"It sounds like you suspect intelligence out there," Kenny said.

"I do. I'm no big Bible person, but I think the jury is still out on more than we care to admit. We pretty much know that the Big Bang occurred. *Why* is still a question yet to be answered."

"I'd like to have a look at the cubes sometime."

"I'll show you afterwhile, providing that your lips are sealed. You're the first person I've told anything about this, other than that I'm experimenting."

"Nary a word," Kenny said, forking up some potato salad. "What's to keep somebody from stealing your invention?" he added.

"I thought of that. I'm no computer science person, but I have pretty sophisticated physics software. I couldn't figure out a way to hide the cube's composition. So I thought, what the heck, I'll ask the computer to do it for me."

"What happened?" Kenny said, turning to his cole slaw.

"It worked."

"How do you know?"

"I ran a series of tests to discover what the stuff is made of. *I* know what it is, but I wanted to know if anybody else could find out."

"And—"

"Zip, *Substance Unknown*."

"Did you build the detector?" Kenny said.

"Yes. It's taken two years to get it working right.

I'm no electrician. I crossed some wires or something the first time and it caught on fire, though only on the inside. I had to build another one—had it built, I should say. A local cabinet maker built it. He used fire resistant glass this time. At least I can look inside and see what's going on, smoke or anything. I did all of the circuitry. I was really nervous about trying it again. Here goes, I said, and hit the switch. Nothing happened for a few moments. Then a green glow appeared. It's really bright and lights up the whole room. It scared the crap out of me. Sodipop barked and ran downstairs and got under a couch."

Kenny laughed and looked at the dog lying near the steps. He was shifting his eyes from one speaker to the other.

"I had bought a fire extinguisher and stood by with it in case there was another fire," Josephine continued. "After about sixty seconds or so the green glow subsided. Sodipop came back upstairs and stared at me. Anyway, I guess it worked this time. I've always been bad about flying by the seat of my pants. It's a miracle I didn't burn this house down. People around the lake are talking about the green glow coming from my lab at night."

"I've heard the rumor," Kenny said.

"What are they saying?"

"Another Frankenstein monster, maybe."

Josephine laughed and said, "Well, I'll just keep them guessing for a while."

"Do you turn Lazarus on every night?" Kenny said.

"Not every night. But when I've experimented with

adjusting the charge, I put the cubes back in to see if I've nulified anything. I haven't. The cubes are still intact ... *Substance Unknown* is still the read out."

"What's causing the green glow?" Kenny said, setting his plate aside and having a drink of beer.

"Photons, I suspect," Josephine said, tossing a rib bone to Sodipop. "When the photons decay, the glow disapates; the particles should actually decay much faster. Lazarus has retarded the process somehow ... violating laws of physics left and right."

The two of them turned to see a young girl coming toward them along the beach. "It's Ellie," Josephine said. "She lives back up the hill. She cleans house for me. Sweet girl, family is very poor." The girl waved and broke into a wide smile. Josephine waved back.

"Does she know about your experiments?" Kenny said, lowering his voice as the girl drew nearer.

"She's seen the glow from my lab a couple of times and asked about it. Just something I'm working on, I told her." Josephine fell silent when the girl approached the steps to the deck.

The girl looked to be in her middle teens. She was slender, slightly knock-kneed as she walked. Her hair, earlob length, was blonde. Large, hazel eyes spoke of an inner maturity born, perhaps, of early responsibility in a household often struggling to make ends meet.

"Hi, Ellie," Josephine said, rising to meet the girl as she crested the steps onto the deck.

"Hi, Miss Holland," the girl said. She shot a look at Kenny then bent down and stroked Sodipop's head. The dog's curly cue tail was switching in greeting the familiar visitor.

"I'd like you to meet my friend Kenny," Josephine said.

Kenny rose from his chair to greet the girl. "It's nice to meet you," the girl said. Kenny took her hand in his and returned the greeting.

"I came to tell you that I have to help my mom with something on Monday," the girl said, releasing Kenny's hand and turning to Josephine. "Is it okay if I come on Tuesday?"

"Of course, dear."

"Are you still experimenting?" the girl said, smiling.

"Oh, you know me, Ellie, always experimenting with something."

"Well, I better get back home before it starts getting dark," the girl said.

"Have you had supper?" Josephine said.

"Not yet."

"Hang on a minute, I'll send these ribs home with you."

"Ok."

Josephine went into the house and shortly returned with two plates, upon one of which she had added heaping portions of potato salad and cole slaw. She had a roll of aluminum foil under one arm. She covered the potato salad and slaw with foil then put several pieces of rib on the other plate and covered it as well.

"Thank you Miss Holland," the girl said when taking the two plates in her hands. "It was nice to meet you," she added, turning to Kenny.

"It was nice meeting you," Kenny said.

When the girl had gone, Josephine said, "She has a younger sister. Mother isn't well, father works at whatever he can find, local sawmills, mostly. I fix her a nice lunch when she comes to clean. She works like a sled dog. I tell her to slow down. She does for a little bit then she's right back. She comes every other week. I pay her $18 an hour."

"Generous," Kenny said.

"She's worth every penny of it," Josephine said. "She wants to do what I do when she grows up, which is kind of nothing, these days, to tell the truth."

"I saw intelligence in her eyes," Kenny said.

"She's whip smart. And she's *so* interested in my experiments. I'm thinking that I might tell her what I'm doing. I think she would keep it our secret if I asked her to."

"By the way, when do I get a demonstration on your bait?" Kenny said.

"How about tomorrow morning? We can take the pontoon down lake to the Palisades; deep water below the bluffs."

"Sounds like a plan."

"Why don't we load my tent into the car and take it to your camp and pitch it before dark?" Josephine said. "Then we can come back and hang out for a while longer, maybe listen to some music over a glass or two of wine. Do you like bluegrass and country?"

"Love it," Kenny said, though he scarcely knew the difference between the two.

"I'll put on some Rhonda Vincent and George Jones, maybe a little Haggard."

"Where did you get that girl Ellie for the story?" Aaron said while he and Amanda took the boat to Pine Cove for more ice and a few grocery items.

"Well, Lt, since you were so tricky about putting me on the spot about what Josephine did with the detector—that you so masterfully built, even if it did catch on fire once—I decided that I might need Ellie to get the truth out of you—well, Josephine, about what the engredients are in that mysterious bait she has made. And now you've really got me stumped with those cubes and what she put in them to catch that 20 pound channelcat."

"We're wading into deep water here, girl," Aaron said as they approached the store's boat dock.

"I'm a good swimmer," Amanda said, hopping out of the boat and securing a line.

"Good, you'll need to when you find out what Josephine is using for the bait."

"I know one thing, she's a good cook ... making me hungry with blackend fish, ribs, margaritas."

"She's your character, pretty much," Aaron said, "so the menu is yours."

"I guess so. Anyway, rich as she is, I don't see her grilling turkey dogs."

"That's our style," Aaron said, chuckling.

Chapter Five

Another thunderstorm hammered the lake during the night. Kenny's tent blew down but not away. The canvass popped like a flag in a gale. Then it collapsed. When the wind eased up, he managed to erect the center polls once more and drive in the stakes that had been ripped from the ground.

At dawn he heard a dog bark. A female voice was close on its heels: "Kenny, are you alright?"

"A little wet is all," he said, pushing the tent flap to one side and exiting.

"Come on back to the house with me," she said, "I'll fix breakfast and you can dry out."

Kenny collected his duffel and some dry clothes. The three of them set out along the beach. "Whew! What a storm!" Josephine said.

"The tent blew down but the two of us managed to stay out of the lake."

After a breakfast of hotcakes and sausage, Josephine went to her lab and returned with a stainless steel box about the size of a small jewelery case.

Embarking onto the pontoon, she took her place behind the wheel and started the outboard. "How far is it?" Kenny said as he had a seat and took Sodipop onto his lap.

"It's a ways but I'll speed things up." She pulled away from the dock and eased the throttle forward. Kenny was surprised at how fast the cumbersome craft could move across the water.

In little less than thirty minutes, Josephine pointed to a collosal span of bluffs ranged along the main channel's southern shoreline. "Palisades up ahead!" she said. The great wall of limestone rose like a fortress, held in base relief by forest that trimmed its crest like garland, then decended in tapering fashion on either end to the water's edge. Kenny could only imagine the panaramic view from such heights. The beauty of this lake isn't often given its due, he thought.

Josephine began to throttle the Merc down and the pontoon settled into the water, leaving behind a deepening wake. Nearing the bluffs, she toyed with the outboard, shifting into reverse from time to time in order to slow her approach. "See that cavity in the rock about four feet up from the water line?" she said.

"Yes."

"There's a kind of ring that's been washed out over a zillion years. You can tie up there."

"Will do," Kenny said, making his way forward and finding the bow line. Josephine skillfully nudged the pontoon into the base of the bluff. Kenny located the ring in the rock and ran the line through it then secured the boat.

Josephine cut the engine as Kenny made his way back to where she was now standing. "I've never measured the water depth here, but I'm guessing it's easily a couple hundred feet or more," she said.

"May not be able to fish the bottom," Kenny said.

"I doubt that we'll need to." Sodipop had taken up a spot high upon the boat's instrument panel. Kenny wondered if the dog knew something he didn't.

Josephine opened a long storage compartment where a rod and reel was stowed. She reached beyond it, however, and picked up a coil of half inch nylon rope. "I'm going to try something different this time and use both of the cubes just to see what happens."

She dropped the coil of rope onto the boat's deck. Kenny guessed it was fifty feet or so. Reaching into the storage compartment once more, she found a pair of scissors and a ball of baling twine. She tied a loop into the end of the nylon rope. Cutting off six exact lengths of twine, she tripled them for strength then tied each with a double knot into the loop, leaving eight or ten inches of the two pieces of twine dangling.

Finding a pair of surgical gloves in the storage compartment, she pulled them on—shooting a look at Kenny—as though she were preparing for surgery. Kenny knelt beside her for closer observation. "The box, please," she said.

"Why the gloves?" Kenny handed the stainless steel box to her.

"I don't want to introduce any of my own chemistry, though I don't know that it would happen—or, matter; just being safe." She opened the box. Sodipop whined and switched his tail.

Inside the container were two cubes, each about the size of an ice cube, though one was slightly larger than the other. They had a greenish tone. Kenny couldn't detect any scent coming from them. "Why is one a little larger than the other?" he said.

"I don't know. Just some clever something Lazarus did, I suppose."

"May I touch them?" Kenny said.

"Yes, better put on some gloves, though."

Josephine handed Kenny a pair of surgical gloves. After he pulled them on, she picked up the box and held it near him. He felt of one, then the other, though he didn't pick them up. He found them slightly warm to the touch through the gloves. "Squeeze them a little," Josephine said. He did so and the cubes caved a bit to his touch then resumed their perfect symmetry. Sodipop barked. "This scares him for some reason," Josephine said.

"He may know something we don't."

"Perhaps," she said, lowering the box onto the boat's deck once more. She picked up one of the cubes and tied it to the end of one of the bundled strings of baling twine, causing the cube to collapse slightly, then double knotting it. She did the same with the remaining cube. "Tie the end of the rope to that rail," she said, pointing to a chrome rail on the boat's port side. When Kenny had secured the line, she pitched the bait into the water about ten feet out.

The two of them took a seat on the storage compartment and watched the line, half of which was floating, descending little by little with the weight of the bait beneath the dark water lapping gently against the bluff.

They had sat for no more than five minutes when Sodipop growled. Josephine cut to him and said, "He hardly ever does that." Those words scarcely escaped her lips when what remained of the floating line suddenly disappeared beneath the surface with such force that it slung water droplets onto the deck of the pontoon. "I think we got a bite," Josephine said.

"Yes, I would say we have," Kenny said, bracing himself when the line's slack was taken up completely and the pontoon lurched sideways.

"Jesus!" Josephine said. Sodipop growled again.

"Let's see if we can haul it in," Kenny said, rising from his seat and taking the line in both hands. He tugged on the line and was met with a powerful resistance that nearly pulled him overboard. "What do you think it is?" he said, turning the line lose and noting that the rope had torn holes in his gloves.

"Gar, maybe," Josephine said.

The pontoon lurched sideways again, more forcefully this time and into the side of the bluff, sending Kenny, Josephine, and Sodipop sprawling onto the deck. "Maybe we better cut it loose," Kenny said, rising to his knees.

"No, I don't want to lose the cubes." She reached and picked up Sodipop.

"Then I think we better untie before the boat gets bashed to pieces," Kenny said just as another lurch sent the boat into the bluff once more.

"Right!"

Kenny crept along the deck and made his way to the bow and quickly untied the boat which immediately began to come about and head toward the main channel.

"Now what?" Kenny said, returning to Josephine and taking Sodipop from her.

"Let's go along for the ride," she said, laughing while the pontoon began picking up speed.

"Hemingway would love this," Kenny said.

"God! What have I done?"

"I don't know, but I think you better start the motor and stand by just in case this thing decides to head for the bluff again."

"Good idea," Josephine said, making her way on unsteady feet to the boat's controls.

Kenny's advice turned out to be prophetic. The boat suddenly went into a 180 degree turn. Josephine put the Merc in reverse but the boat seemed hell bent for the bluff. "I think it wants to slam us again! Probably trying to get leverage and break loose!" Josephine said.

"Why the hell doesn't it just let go? There's no hook!"

"I don't know!" Josephine said above the roar of the outboard.

"More throttle!" Kenny said. Josephine eased the throttle forward and the outboard's prop began to churn the water near the transom, to no measurable results. "More!"

Josephine had the Merc nearly wide open. Perhaps

whatever was towing them was getting tired. At any rate the boat made a 60 degree turn and headed away from the bluff. Josephine shifted the motor back into neutral. She shot a look at Kenny and blew out her cheeks in relief. "If this thing decides to sound, it may take us to the bottom with it."

"That baling twine won't take it, thank God," Kenny said.

The pontoon set a more or less steady course back into the main channel. "I think it's taking us home," Josephine said.

"Looks that way," Kenny said, handing Sodipop to her.

"I wish it would surface so that we can see what it is."

"I suspect we'll find out soon enough."

Forty minutes later Gravois Mills came into view. They had met—or, passed a handful of boaters but no one seemed to notice that the pontoon was being towed. Kenny and Josephine smiled and waved at passersby, drawing their attention away from the taunt line off the boat's port bow.

Kenny looked to the sturn to see if any boats were trailing in the pontoon's wake. That's when he heard Josephine gasp. He cut to her then to where she was pointing. A fish—two of them—had begun to surface, showing only dorsal fins at first, then all of their length for just a moment before submerging. The creatures looked to be nearly half as long as the pontoon. "Bluecat!" Josephine cried.

Sodipop whined and hopped to the top of the boat's instrument panel.

"Holy crap!" Kenny returned. "What do you think they weigh?"

"I didn't see their underbelly, so I wouldn't try to guess. The record is something like 150 pounds. I've never seen a photo of any this long, though. They may hit 300 pounds each or more."

"What are we going to do with them?" Kenny said.

"If we get home with them, and it looks like we will, seeing that they don't appear to have any intention of turning the bait loose, we'll kill and dress them out and have one hell of a fish fry."

"Kill them—how?"

Josephine reached into a compartment near the boat's steering wheel and found a snub-nosed .38. "We'll put a bullet—well, maybe a couple into their heads."

"What will you tell neighbors, I mean how they were caught?" Kenny said.

"Worms, I guess."

As the pontoon was drawn to within a hundred feet of Josephine's dock, Kenny said, "I think we better try and coax those things to surface and shoot them. If we get too close to the dock and they get under it, getting them out could be a problem."

"Good idea."

"Put the motor in reverse and see if you can angle us toward the shore and shallower water."

"Right," she said, shifted the Merc into reverse and turning the wheel clockwise, easing the throttle forward

slowly. The fish resisted, but less so. Josephine was suc-
ceding in backing the boat toward shore, a good hundred feet south of the dock. She checked the .38 for
shells then handed it to Kenny. He stood along the
boat's port rails and watched for dorsal fins.

When the boat had reached encreasingly shallow
water some fifteen or twenty feet from the shore, the
fish's backs began to surface. When their heads appeared, Josephine cried, "Go for it!"

Kenny held the pistol with both hands, aimed and
fired three shots in quick succession. One bullet missed
its target but the other two went home in the back of
the fishs' heads. They thrashed violently for a moment
then turned loose of the bait. Settling into bloodied water, the fish began floating off shore. "We'll lose them if
they get into deep water!" Josephine said.

"Not if I can help it!" Kenny said. He laid the .38
down and jumped overboard into four feet of water. He
struggled to the fish and grabbed gills with both hands,
straining to drag the fish to shore. Josephine quickly ran
the pontoon's bow onto the bank, cut the engine and
jumped overboard to assist.

Neighbors who had heard the gun shots were making their way along the beach. Some were running.
Kenny had both hands in one of the fish's gill, Josephine
the other, and they slowly dragged both fish into shallow water until they rested on the bottom. "What in the
world!" one woman said, putting a hand to her mouth
and cutting to her husband.

"What are they?" cried another.

"Bluecat," Josephine said breathlessly, extracting

her hands from the fish's gill.

"Where did you catch them?" someone asked.

"Along the bluffs at Palisades," Kenny said, turning his fish loose and washing his hands in the lake.

"What'd you use?" a man asked, drawing near and gazing along the fish's shocking length.

"Worms," Josephine said, glancing at Kenny who concurred with a nod.

"What do you think they weigh?" another in the crowd asked.

"Could hit 300 pounds each," Kenny offered.

"What you gonna do with them?" asked a young boy.

"Clean them. We could use some help," Josephine said. "Big fish fry. Spread the word."

While the crowd stood by the fish, Josephine and Kenny excused themselves to get out of their wet, bloodied clothes and have a quick shower. Kenny found a change of clothes in his tent.

Having gotten cleaned up and into dry clothes, the two of them returned to their catch. Josephine brought along a camera and a number of photos were taken. One of the men in the crowd said that he knew a fellow back in the hills that raised hogs. He had a scale that could be hooked to a tree limb. The fish could be weighed in that way. He called the man and thirty minutes later he arrived in a pickup. He whistled when he saw the two fish lying in shallow water. The scale was hooked over a limb of a nearby oak tree and its line ran through the mouth of one of the fish and out a gill. After it was weighed, the same was done with the second fish. The first fish weighed in at 300 pounds; the other, 325 pounds.

Josephine, Kenny and others handy with a knife set to cleaning the fish and filleting the meat. Working alongside Josephine, Kenny leaned into her and nodded toward the line still dangling from the pontoon. The bait had settled to the bottom. "Better get the bait out of the water before something else gets them," Kenny said softly. Josephine laid her knife down, wadded into the water and clandestinely found the two cubes lying on the bottom in two feet of water. Keeping her body between those who were busy and chatting while they worked on the fish, she gathered up the line and laid it and the cubes on the deck of the boat and covered them with a seat cushion. When the fish cleaning was done she would return the cubes to the stainless steel box. She noted, when lifting the cubes from the water, that neither had been damaged by the fish's jaws.

"How many worms did you put on the hooks to catch fish like this?" someone asked who had noticed the line being retrieved from the water.

"Oh, several," Josephine said, casting a look at Kenny who only smiled as he cut away a fillet of meat from the fish's rib cage. Sodipop, lying in the shade of the tree where the fish had been weighed, barked and switched his curly cue tail. Word spread rapidly regarding Josephine's monster fish. Their meat would be featured at her annual fish fry on the first Saturday in June, weather permitting. Of course she hadn't room in her freezer to accomadate all of the fish; a number of folk offered to store the remainder until the day of the fish fry.

"Did you go a little overboard with fish that size, Amanda, and *two* on the same line?" Aaron said while his partner rummaged about in the ice chest in search of cream cheese for bagels from Pine Cove Store.

"You had Josephine and Lazarus create *two* of those cubes. Might as well go the whole nine yards and land some whoppers."

"You did that," Aaron said, pouring coffee. "It scared the bejesus out of Sodipop."

Amanda laughed while she spread cream cheese on bagels for herself and Aaron. "I'm having more fun with that dog. I wish he could talk. I wonder what he would say."

"This is crazy, folks," Aaron said, taking a bagel and handing a cup of coffee to Amanda.

"I have a feeling it's going to get a lot crazier," Amanda said, "especially when you reveal what those cubes are made of. Any hints?"

"Not yet," Aaron said, biting into his bagel.

"I don't think all of the neighbors are buying the worms."

"I wouldn't," Aaron said.

Chapter Six

Those who lived nearest to Josephine and who had, on occasion, seen the greenish glow coming from the top floor of her home weren't so sure that the fish had been caught on nothing but run of the mill worms. They good naturedly questioned her about the possibility of there being something special about the worms. "A worm is a worm," she returned, smiling, and looking to Kenny for support which he happily gave. He wondered, though, how much longer she could keep the nature of her experiments secret. If word got out about what had taken place in her mini detector, half the particle physicists in the world might show up at her door, not to mention a flood of reporters converging on tiny Gravois Mills.

Kenny was no physicist, but he had his own theory. He suspected that his new friend had one of her own, though keeping it to herself, for now. Seeing that both fish exceeded the known record for bluecat by at least 150 pounds, he wondered if the *bait* had caused a shockingly rapid growth metamorphosis in the two fish once they had come in contact with the bait.

She had caught a 20 pound channelcat with the same bait, Kenny considered. There was nothing unusual about that fish's size, of course, for record channelcat were known to reach 80 pounds or more. But she had caught the 20 pounder before "fiddling"—as she put it—with the detector's energy level. She said that she elevated the output. At any rate, something extraordinary must have happened inside the detector. Bingo! Mind boggling, subatomic sythesis; intriguing, to say the least. Something troubled him, however: Could *eating* the fish be dangerous? Kenny thought that he had better pitch his theory to professor Holland.

"What you're suggesting has crossed my mind," Josephine said over dinner. "As for whether or not eating the fish could be dangerous, I think not. The channelcat we ate was caught in the same way. I felt no ill effects. Did you?"

"No," Kenny said, "but you said that you've adjusted the detector's output since then."

"I did."

"Could there be any radio activity?"

"The detector would have registered any if present."

"What if everybody at the fish fry gets morphed?"

Josephine laughed and said, "Well, you have a point even if it is far fetched."

"I wonder if we should cook a bit of the fish and try it out before feeding it to others," Kenny said.

"Ginnie pigs?"

"Something like that."

"I wish I had never started screwing around with something like this," Josephine said, drawing a deep breath and releasing it slowly.

"You've kind of got your wagon in the middle of the river, commited to the fish fry."

"I always bought farmed fish before."

"Can't back out now," Kenny said.

"I suppose you're right," Josephine said, rising and refreshing their wine glasses. "When should we do it?"

"No time like the present."

"Who goes first—the first bite, I mean," Josephine said.

"We'll do it together."

"Is that an invitation?" Josephine said, raising her wine glass and gazing at Kenny over its rim.

"It depends on how the fish turns out," Kenny said, smiling and sampling his own wine.

Two days ahead of the annual fish fry, Josephine fetched a fillet of the fish from her deep freeze. "Fry or bake?" she said, flourishing the fillet.

"Fry, I suppose," Kenny said.

"Josephine salted the fish, rolled it in cornmeal then found a skillet.

Sodipop licked his lips and swished his tail.

"I hope I'm not making an orphan of him," Josephine said.

When the fish was ready, she divided the meat and served it on saucers. Shredding a bit of it in search of bones, she then gave some to Sodipop. She and Kenny sat and stared at the fillet, then at each other. "On three," Josephine said. Each of them took the first bite. They rolled their eyes as they chewed, as though trying to detect any immediate affect the fish might be having on them. "How do you feel?" Josephine said, then glancing at Sodipop to see if he was the same size.

"Like going for a swim."

"Be serious."

"I feel fine."

"It's delicious," Josephine said.

"Scrumptious."

"I suppose we better wait until morning before we give it a green light."

"Good idea. If you see my legs sticking out of the tent and down to the water, you'll know something has gone terribly wrong."

They finished their glasses of wine then said goodnight. They laughed, saying that they hoped to see each other in the morning and wearing the same size of clothes that hadn't been ripped to shreds like the Incredible Hulk.

Both Ginnie pigs had trouble falling asleep. They fought off paranoria at every slight physical sensation, wondering if it was the wine—having finished the bottle—or the onslaught of some dire affect from eating the fish. Kenny crawled from his tent a couple of times and walked the beach for a few yards. Josephine slept fully dressed on a couch. She too got up a couple of times, walked out on the deck, looked at a clock, then lay back down.

Dawn arrived and found Josephine and her accomplace alive, if not well rested. Kenny made his way to Josephine's house. She was standing on the deck awaiting his arrival. They gave each other a high five when he crested the steps. Over breakfast they gave the fish a green light. "I'm wondering if you should consider returning the detector's energy setting to its pre-bluecat setting, you know, where it was when you caught the 20 pound channelcat," Kenny said. "Do you remember the setting?" he added.

"I do," Josephine said, adding syrup to her hotcakes. "Why, though? She handed the syrup bottle to Kenny.

"If you plan to do more fishing, and you land something else as large—or, larger, it may get the attention of more than local folk..." Kenny's voice trailed off when Josephine's cell phone rang. She excused herself and picked up the phone lying on a nearby end table.

"Dr. Holland?" the caller said.

"Yes."

"I'm Jim Streeter with *The Kansas City Star*."

"Yes, Mr. Streeter—how did you get my number?"

"Tipster. I understand that you recently caught a couple of fish, bluecat, I believe, of remarkable size."

"I did," Josephine said, rolling her eyes to Kenny. She found a pen and pad and wrote *The Kansas City Star* and held it up for Kenny to read. After a few polite moments of listening to the reporter, Josephine said, "I'll pass on an interview, Mr. Streeter. I'm terribly busy right now."

The conversation ended. Josephine turned to Kenny and said, "I doubt that I've heard the last of this."

"Probably not," Kenny said, taking up his coffee cup. "I wouldn't be surprised to see the fellow at your fish fry."

The annual fish fry was its usual success. What *was* unusual, however, was the crowd that gathered, understandably, given the news of their neighbor's remarkable catch. More than a few hinted, jokingly, at there being a possible link between the two giant bluecat and Josephine's laboratory.

She had driven her car to the church and picked up Evelyn. Expecting the old woman to walk through the woods then manage the steep decline to the pontoon would have been too much. During the drive back to her house, Josephine asked Evelyn if she had seen Marvin lately. "Not for a while," she said. "I hear his banjo sometimes when the wind is coming in my direction."

"I hope he shows up for the fish fry," Josephine said.

Ellie and her family were present, Carl Jenkins as well on whose property Kenny had first camped. Josephine's sister drove in from Sedalia. She was divorced and her one child was visiting the father. Kenny was introduced to her. Some suspected that the girl, cleaning house for Josephine, might be privy to a strange development on the home's top floor. "Miss Holland looks for space stuff" is all Ellie would say. That was, in fact, all she knew at the moment.

Who the tipster was that placed a call to the *Star* didn't concern Josephine. And, too, such a story wouldn't do the lake's tourism any harm. Anglers might flock to the lake in hopes of landing something even close to Josephine's catch.

Mr. Jim Streeter of *The Kansas City Star* was in attendance. Though he hadn't introduced himself to anyone, as yet, he somehow looked like a reporter. He was wearing camo shorts, New Balance tee shirt and Niki sneakers. He might have blended in better had it not been for his turtle shell eyeglasses and notepad protruding from the waistband of his shorts. "Our Mr. Streeter from the *Star*, I'm guessing," Josephine said, nodding toward the young man now in line for a plate of fish.

"Yes, he does have a correspondence look about him," Kenny said. He had noticed Josephine looking about the crowd several times and he asked, "Who are you looking for?"

"Marvin. He lives back in the hills, not far from Evelyn. He keeps to himself. But I was hoping he would show up today, maybe bring his banjo. God, can he play that thing! If he wasn't such a hermit, he could make it in Nashville."

"Does he work somewhere?" Kenny asked.

"He helps out in sawmills now and then when they need him. Otherwise he kind of lives off the land. He's sort of different. Maybe you can meet him sometime."

The reporter was served a fillet of fish. Baked beans, potato salad and sweet iced tea had been catered from a restaurant in Camdenton. He casually strolled to where Josephine, Kenny, and Evelyn were sitting, suggesting that he had picked Josephine out of the crowd even before being served. "His antena is out, here he comes," Josephine said. She, Kenny, Evelyn and Josephine's sister had been served earlier and they sat beneath a cottonwood on the beach no more than ten feet from the water's edge. Josephine's sister was brunette, short and dumpy. Though she was rather quiet, she seemed pleasant. Evelyn didn't talk much either but she seemed to be very much enjoying the meal and gathering. Kenny suspected that living in the old church back in the woods could get pretty lonely at times. She was a tiny thing, rather stooped over, and her hair was white with strands of yellow here and there. Her eyes were blue as the sky above this day.

"Beautiful afternoon for a fish fry," the reporter from the *Star* said, stopping where the group sat. Kenny judged the fellow to be in his middle to late thirties. He sampled his fish and looked out onto the lake and a moderate chop, some of which was produced by boats passing slowly through the cove while those aboard looked to shore and the sizeable picnic.

"It is indeed, Mr. Streeter," Josephine ventured.

The young man smiled and said, "Do I look that obvious?"

"It's the eyeglasses and notepad," Kenny said. "Have a seat," he added.

The reporter found a spot beneath the cottonwood. Josephine introduced him to Kenny, her sister, and Evelyn. He set his paper plate on his lap then said, "How many pounds did those two fish dress out to anyway?"

"Actually, we didn't weigh it when the filleting was done," Josephine said. "But as you can see, there's plenty to go around," she added, glancing to where a half dozen volunteers were cooking and serving fish. Behind them was a square of plywood nailed to a tree. Josephine had mounted a number of photos taken of the two fish the day they were caught.

After finishing a bite of potato salad and chewing it thoughtfully, Streeter said, "How in the world did two fish of that size get caught on *one* little hook?"

"Two hooks," Josephine lied. "One above the other," she added, figuring she might as well tell a bigger lie while she was at it. She disliked the deceit, but Streeter had to be kept at bay. Josephine's sister coughed and rolled her eyes to Evelyn.

The reporter clucked his tongue and shook his head. "It's a wonder you didn't get pulled overboard," he said, picking up his cup of tea.

"Yes, it's a wonder," Josephine said, glancing at Kenny.

"A wonder for sure," Kenny agreed.

Evelyn was quietly listening to the conversation while she enjoyed her fish. She smiled slightly from time to time, as though she knew something that Streeter didn't. She didn't, though, but having lived on the lake for so many years she was suspicious of plain old worms being the bait that Josephine used. And she had heard the talk of a strange, green glow coming from the top floor of her house.

"How many worms on those hooks?" Streeter asked, cutting to Josephine then her sister while he set his tea down and had a bite of fish.

"Oh, gobs."

"Delicious fish, Dr. Holland," Streeter said, getting to his feet and strolling off toward the crowd.

"I don't think he bought the worms," Josephine said.

"Probably not—I wouldn't," Kenny said.

"Neither would I," Evelyn said.

"Why?"

"Not complicated enough coming from a physicist," Kenny said, forking potato salad and casting a look at Evelyn. "Anyway, if he did buy the worms, he suspects you did something to them."

"Like what?"

"I'm only a mechanical engineer," Kenny said, "how should I know?"

Jim Streeter from the *Star* got himself a second helping of fish then moved away from the crowd and strolled a few yards down the beach. Noting that he wasn't being observed, he withdrew a Baggie from his pocket and placed a portion of the fish in it.

The fish fry ended just before dusk. People began to disperse, some by cars and pickups, others in small fishing boats whose bows had been drawn onto shore. Several volunteers, including Ellie, remained to help with the clean up. Working beside Josephine who was wiping down a folding table, Ellie leaned into her and whispered, "Did you really catch those two big fish on worms?"

Josephine glanced about, noting that Jim Streeter from the *Star* was gone, and whispered back, "No. I'll tell you sometime if you can keep a secret."

Ellie smiled and nodded. "I've never told a secret in my *whole* life, Miss Holland."

"I don't know how much longer I can wait for you to tell me what Josephine used for that bait," Amanda said as she and Aaron made their way toward the old church that she wanted to see.

"Well, we're getting close and she's got an investigative reporter on her trail now. I like what you did with Kenny and Josephine deciding to test the fish before feeding it to others."

"When are those two going to make love?" Amanda said as she and Aaron reached the church and began mounting the short flight of steps.

"Well, like I said, she's your character. I'll let you decide how coy you want her to be."

"What's *The Kansas City Star* reporter going to do with that piece of fish he secretly put in a Baggie?" Amanda said.

"You're about to find out."

"Since Marvin didn't show up at the fish fry," Amanda said, "when do we get to meet him and hear some banjo?"

"Soon, and I think the lonely fellow needs a girlfriend."

"I'll fix him up," Amanda said.

Chapter Seven

Dr. Kaitland Porter sat at her desk in her office on the second floor of the California Institute of Metamorphic Biology (CIMB). Dr. Porter was in her early sixties, married, the mother of three grown children. She was CIMB's director and her plush office reflected her position of importance. She could not be called an attractive woman, by most standards, but as soon as she opened her mouth in conversation her obvious intelligence immediately swept attention away from her rather mousy appearance. She dressed casually. Her work was meticulous.

It was *6:30 a.m.* on a Monday morning. Nothing new had been morphing of late and Dr. Porter was bored, had been for weeks. She drew a deep breath, released it slowly and entwined her fingers before her on her desk. The scent of brewing coffee—100% Columbian beans which she had ground—was beginning to drift lazily across the room, like fog pushed along a forest floor by slight early morning breeze. "Hurry up, damnit," she mumbled, cutting to the laboring coffee maker. This is the problem with grinding ones own beans, she mused. More natural oil, takes water longer to leach down. Worth the wait, though, she concluded.

Upon arriving at her office a little after six, she had collected a message on her office phone: UPS was to deliver an early package, perishable, on dry ice. Unusual, such a delivery, though she had once gotten a birthday gift sent in such a way from her daughter in San Francisco: chocolate covered strawberries, huge things.

The coffee was ready and Dr. Porter fetched a cup, added a touch of coffee creamer to the tar black brew and returned to her desk. She set the cup down gently when she heard a knock on the door. She rose and opened to UPS; early even for them, she thought. The package was the size of a shoebox, Styrofoam, and taped securely shut. She signed for the package and returned to her desk, noting a return address on the package as she strode arosss the carpeted room: Jim Streeter, *The Kansas City Star*. Probably not strawberries, she thought as she sat down, sampled her coffee once more then took up a pair of scissors. An envelope was taped to the top of the box's lid. She cut it loose, put an opener to it and extracted a letter from Mr. Jim Streeter.

Dear Dr. Porter: Please find enclosed sample of what I think may be of interest to you. It is a fillet—part of one, I should say, for I ate half of it and found it to be quite good—of a 300 pound catfish caught on central Missouri's Lake of the Ozarks.

In addition to this particular fish being 150 pounds beyond a record catch of bluecat, two fish of this remarkable size were hooked on a single line, 2 hooks, one above the other, so I was told. *The fisherman, Josephine Holland, a gorgeous strawberry blonde holding PhDs in particle physics and molecular biology said that she caught the fish with worms. I for one am suspicious of that explanation, given widespread talk around the lake that she has been conducting experiments in her laboratory on the top floor of her lakehouse. Locals say that they have seen a greenish glow coming from her lab at night on more than one occasion.*

I'm wondering, Dr. Porter, if you might care to examine the contents of this box to see if something out of the ordinary has been in play that would account for 625 pounds—both fish—of bluecat to be caught in such a way that Ms. Holland Described.—Sincerely, Jim Streeter.

Dr Porter laid the letter aside and took up scissors once more and cut away the tape that sealed the box. Removing the lid, she was met with a cloud of vapor from the dry ice. Lying at the bottom of the box was the fillet of fish, ensconced in a Baggie. She rose from behind her desk, picked up the box and carried into an adjoining room that served as a small lab. There, she donned a pair of surgical gloves and removed the specimen from atop the dry ice. She undid the twisty that secured the Baggie and extracted the fillet. It should thaw before I put it under a microscope, she thought. She considered nuking it but didn't want to risk disrupting anything that might othewise be detectable, what that could be she had no clue, as yet. To hasten things some, she stacked a few books beneath a table lamp then placed the specimen on top near the bulb.

Returning to her desk, Dr. Porter warmed her coffee and sat back down. She turned in her swivel chair and looked out onto Malibu beach. There was something therapeutic about watching the waves roll in; millions of years of repetition, bringing one grain of coral at a time to shore. It made her world seem almost intollerably small. That thought depressed her now and she turned away from the window, sampled her coffee again and wondered how much longer the fish would need to thaw. The dry ice had rendered it hard as granite, though it wasn't particularly thick. Weird, a half eaten piece of catfish sent to her from a reporter in Kansas City. He must be as bored as her. She might have pitched the thing into the trash were it not so ridiculous. Funny how obsurdities had a way of hooking her; pathetic grasping for something new in a field where nothing seemed new anymore. Biology has gotten too predictable, she thought, raising her coffee cup to her lips. She found that the brew had grown lukewarm again. How long had she been in la la land? She should check on the fish.

The fillet hadn't thawed entirely, but Dr. Porter wasn't in a mood for waiting any longer. She put it under a mircoscope, adjusted the lens and peered at what lay before her on the 3x3 piece of glass. "Looks like a piece of fish to me," she said, as though an assistant were standing beside her. She adjusted the scope for looking deeper into the fish's tissue. She blinked once, rubbed her eyes then had another look. What she saw upon closer examination was what appeared to be some abnormality in a fragment of rib bone shattered by the filleting knife. The piece of bone had an odd, greenish coloring that seemed out of concert with the surrounding flesh. Adjusting the scope's focus once more, Dr. Porter blinked a couple of times when she saw the greenish spot move a centimeter away from the fragment of bone.

Removing the fish from beneath the scope, she strode along the counter where she was working and placed the specimen beneath a more powerful, state of the art scope. Swimming before her eyes was something she couldn't identify. I'm no physicist, she thought, but this thing looks like a Higgs boson particle that half the world has been talking about, or something that's mimicking it. It's just swimming there with zero spin. What's it doing in a piece of catfish for heaven's sake? She reached for a power cord and plugged it into a port in the side of the scope. She stepped to one side to a desktop computer and began to type search instructions: Identify zero spin particle in fish.

She sat staring at the computer screen and awaiting an answer.

Please repeat and rephrase question.

Dr. Porter thought for a moment then began typing again: Zero spin particle in fish. What is it?

She sat and waited once more. Impatient for an answer, she was about to retype the question when the computer responded:

Particle unknown. Has been introduced from exotic source.

Dr. Porter mulled over the response. Fine hairs at her temples trembled slightly. She felt a chill run up her arms and onto the back of her neck. She returned to the scope and removed the specimen then strode to a refrigerator and placed it within.

Returning to her office she placed a call to *The Kansas City Star* and asked to speak to Jim Streeter. Getting him, the conversation was rather short. She would forward the computer's answer to Streeter's laptop.

Kenny had a standing invitation for a shower and breakfast at Josephine's place. He didn't want to wear out his welcome and only took her up on it from time to time. Some mornings he just showed up for coffee, having had an early swim in the lake. This morning he got dressed, washed his face in the lake and brushed his teeth with clean drinking water. Nights were still warm. He slept on top of his sleeping bag and in his underwear. Usually in the wee hours of the morning he reached for a light blanket.

Exiting the tent, he set out along the beach with his laptop bag slung over one shoulder. Josephine's house was wired for Internet. He needed to pay some bills online. He was thinking more and more that he might remain camped on the lake until late fall, if his host didn't reposes her tent. He had called his renters in Kansas City and asked them to let him know if there were any problems at his place, conveniently next door to them. He had a mail slot in his front door, so mail dropped into the foyer wouldn't be a problem, and there wouldn't be much; virtually all of his bills were paperless these days. He didn't anticipate any parcel deliveries.

Josephine was an early riser. She was sitting on the deck with a cup of coffee. Sodipop was nearby, finishing his splash of Coke in a saucer. He looked up and licked his whiskers as Kenny mounted the steps. The dog barked once, announcing the visitor's arrival. "Good morning," Josephine said.

"Good morning to you," Kenny returned.

"How about some coffee? I made cinnamon rolls early this morning."

"Sounds good. I need to pay a couple of bills. Mind if I connect?" Kenny said, unslinging his laptop bag from his shoulder.

"Be my guest. There's an outlet right there." She pointed to a socket near the table were she was sitting.

After getting online and paying his condo untility bill and insurance for his Tahoe, Kenny shut the laptop down and enjoyed a cup of coffee and roll that Josephine brought to him.

It was a little after eight o'clock when Ellie arrived. The girl liked coffee and Josephine got her a cup as well as a cinnamon roll. "Do I get to see the experiment today?" Ellie said, putting a fork to her roll.

"Yes, when you're done cleaning we'll have lunch then go to my lab."

Ellie finished her roll then took her coffee cup inside and began cleaning. "I hope I don't regret this?" Josephine said. "She's just the smartest little thing and loves science. I want to encourage her any way I can."

"She'll be getting an inside track to what may turn

out to be a scientific bombshell," Kenny said.

"There's no turning back now. But I regret fooling around with something like this. I should have found a good book to keep bordom at bay. Now I've got a reporter on my tail and God knows who else will come snooping around next."

"Maybe something good will come of it," Kenny said, reaching with one hand and stroking Sodipop's head.

"Six hundred plus pounds of catfish so far," Josephine said, laughing. "Damn! It was so good!"

"Scrumptious!"

Ellie finished cleaning at eleven o'clock. Josephine fixed egg salad sandwiches and blackberry cobbler for dessert, one of which she had sent home with Evelyn after the fish fry. When the meal was over, the four of them—Sodipop included—made their way to the lab. Ellie could scarcely conceal her excitement with a perpetual smile as they mounted the stairs.

In the lab Ellie and Kenny took a seat on stools at Josephine's work counter. The detector sat nearby. Ellie pursed her lips, drew a deep breath and released it slowly then folded her hands in her lap. She glanced at Kenny, gauging his anticipation.

Reaching inside a cabinet below the counter, Josephine brought out the stainless steel container. She once more donned surgical gloves then handed a pair to Ellie. "You'll need those, dear, if you want to touch them."

Sodipop crept into a corner of the room.

Josephine opened the box. Ellie craned her neck to see inside. "You may touch them." Josephine said.

"What's in these things?" Ellie said.

"Just some stuff I came up with."

"What kind of stuff?" Ellie pursued.

"Secret," Josephine said, "but I'll let you see the detector running. She set the cubes to one side.

After programing the machine, she pushed the start buttom and the detector began to hum, slowly accelerating to a rather high pitch.

"What's it doing?" Ellie said.

"It's searching for sub-atomic particles" Josephine said.

A green glow had risen in the detector. Sodipop whined from his spot across the room. The dog blinked serveral times and switched his tail.

Josephine sat down on a stool in front of the detector and watched physics equation scrowl across the forty-two inch screen suspended before them.

"I don't see Einstein's famous equation," Kenny said.

"You won't," Josephine said. "This has nothing to do with the curvature of space," she added, laughing softly and not taking her eyes off the data crawling across the screen.

"It looks like the tracks chickens make when they've been on our porch after it rains," Ellie said.

Kenny and Josephine laughed.

"How long does it take?" Ellie asked

"Only a few minutes," Josephine said.

A message began to scrowl across the screen:

Particles have not been detected.

Josephine began to type: Thank you. Just showing a friend how you work.

Ellie giggled

Have you further need of me at this time?

No.

Very well.

The three of them sat quietly. Nearing 60 seconds, the detector's humming began to slow. Ellie shifted expectantly on her stool then cast a look at Kenny then Sodipop who was crouched in the corner of the room, as though he anticipated leaving at any moment.

Josephine opened the detector's door. Ellie and Kenny left their stools and hovered near the detector and peered inside. "There's nothing inside," Ellie said.

"Not this time, sweetie."

Kenny bent at the waist and had a closer look inside the machine. He saw a harness of wires that reached an apex where they all were neatly soldered. Being a mechanical engineer by profession, he drew nearer, almost sticking his head inside the machine. "How did you come up with this?"

"Brainstorming with basic physics," Josephine said. "I told you that it caught on fire once."

"Oh my," Ellie said, putting a hand to her mouth.

"I had to rebuild it, as I told you earlier, and redo the circuitry."

Kenny noticed a single, lavender colored wire that hadn't been soldered into place with the others. "What's this?" he said, not touching the wire, only pointing to it.

"Just an extra wire," Josephine said. "I saw no need

for it, so I left it alone."

"Maybe you should connect it," Kenny said, still bent at the waist and gazing up and down the intricate bundle of wiring.

"I don't know if we should," Josephine said. "What if there's another fire?"

"Is the extinguisher fully charged?" Kenny said, glancing at the red tubular thing sitting on the end of the counter.

"Yes."

"I think you should connect the wire, Miss Holland," Ellie said, moving up against Kenny and having a closer look at the machine's inards.

"I agree," Kenny said.

"Alright, but if I burn the house down you two are to blame." Josephine fetched a soldering iron and roll of solder. She plugged the iron in and let it heat for a few moments. She asked Kenny to hold the wire in place that was to be soldered. He did so and Josephine applied solder to the copper tip of the lavender colored wire. A small, acrid plume of smoke rose from where the connection had been made.

With the wire soldered into place among the others at the apex of the harness, Josephine said, "I'll put the cubes inside and do a simple composition test. I've done it before."

Ellie folded her hands in front of her like a church steeple: "Dear God, please don't let Miss Holland's house burn down—Amen."

Josephine began typing: Run simple composition test, please.

The detector began to hum once more. After long moments a message began to crawl across screen: *You have alterered original circuitry ... must resubmit...*

Josephine began to type equation and Kenny and Ellie watched it race across the screen like Wall Street ticker tape.

When she had finished resubmitting, Josephine took a deep breath and released it with a rush, blowing out her cheeks as she shot a look at her two accomplices. Sodipop was under a chair now. "I doubt that Einstein or Peter Higgs would approve of this," she said. She clicked on the start button.

Kenny passed a hand across his brow and cast a look at Josephine, as though he suspected that he had screwed up everything.

A familiar greenish glow began to light the glass. Then it turned to purple, then red, and back to green. Text began to crawl across the computer's screen: *You have circumvented certain laws of physics and biology.*

Violate them? Josephine typed in response.

No. You have circumvented them.

End run? she typed.

Yes, you could say that.

What is the risk? Josephine typed.

No further data available...

Josephine started to open the detector's door then hesitated. "I'm afraid to look inside."

Kenny got off of his stool and stepped to the detector. He attempted to open the door but it wouldn't unlock. He put his face near the detector's glass and peered inside. "We've only got *one* cube now, larger than the others." He looked to Josephine and her face had blanched. "What's happened?" he said.

"Maybe a ghost did it," Ellie said. "My grandma said they can do stuff."

Josephine smiled at Ellie's words then began typing code that unlocked the detector's door. "What happened in there?" Kenny said.

"I don't know at the moment."

It was *1:00 a.m.* and the California Institute of Metamorphic Biology was mostly darkend; only Dr. Kaitland Porter's lab was lit. With rather vacant eyes she stared at her computer screen. An empty coffee cup sat next to the keyboard. She picked it up and swirled the little bit that remained at the bottom. Putting the cup to her lips and noting that the coffee was cold, she set the cup back down.

She had scarcely moved from her seat at the computer since the building had closed, with a single exception of going to the bathroom then making a peanut butter and jelly sandwich. A small blob of strawberry jelly dropped onto the laptop's keyboard. "Damnit," she mumbled, then found a tissue and cleaned the tops and between F and G keys.

Dr. Porter had typed inquiry after inquiry into the computer regarding what had been used to catch the fish sent to her by Jim Streeter of *The Kansas City Star*. The program responded with the same answer over and over: *Unknown... appears to have undergone concealing technology presently unaccounted for...*

She rose from her chair and strode across the lab. She looked at the fillet of fish she had extracted from the refrigerator. Pulling on surgical gloves, she placed the specimen under a microscope. Extracting a steril scalpel from its wrapper, she exposed a blood vessel that she believed had been located near the fish's spinal column. Fetching steril tweezers, she removed the blood vessel then sent it through the same series of tests that the fish had undergone when she had received it from Streeter. She took her seat at the computer once more and began to type: *Identify composition of specimen.*

She drew a deep breath and released it with a rush, glancing at her watch. It was *3:00 a.m.* She folded her hands in her lap and waited. She straightened abruptly, as though she had heard a door slam. The computer was responding: *DNA found.*

Well isn't that special, she thought. Fish *do* have DNA. She typed: fish?

Human ... female.

She began typing almost frantically: Please deepen analysis.

She waited.

Unclasified sub-atomic particle infiltrated DNA.

From what source? Dr. Porter typed.

Unknown.

Putting the fish back into the refrigerator, Dr. Porter returned to her desk, picked up her cell phone and placed a call to Jim Streeter at *The Kansas City Star*. She glanced at her watch: it was *3:30 a.m.* That would put Kansas City's central time a couple hours later. She hoped Streeter was an early riser. He was it appeared for when he answered he sounded wide awake. She could hear water running and the clink of glass, making coffee she supposed. "Hello, Dr. Porter." He must have added her name and number to his phone's list, she guessed.

"Mr. Streeter, forgive me for calling you at this hour."

"No problem."

"I ran more tests on the fish you sent me. I think you'll be interested in what I found."

"Shoot."

"DNA was found in a blood vessel."

"Fish have DNA don't they?" Streeter said.

"Yes, of course. But this is human DNA."

"Mermaid?"

Dr. Porter didn't respond and was wondering if Streeter was something of an inherent smart aleck. "*Human* DNA. An unclasified sub-atomic particle infiltrated it somehow."

"You've lost me." Streeter's tone had become much more serious.

"I think the particle morphed the fish, who knows what else."

"How?"

"Source unknown is all the computer told me."

"I think there's little question regarding the source," Streeter said.

"Miss Holland?"

"Exactly. She was elusive about how she caught the fish. She has degrees in particle physics and molecular biology," Streeter said.

"Bingo."

"She struck me as an out-of-the-box type. She has a friend, nice fellow. I did a little investigation on him. He's a mechanical engineer."

"Bingo."

"I think the two of them have engineered something way the *hell* out of the box," Streeter said. "I'm going back down there and snoop around a little more."

"Let me know what you turn up."

"Will do—Dr. Porter"

"Yes."

"Don't let this leak."

"Nary a word."

"Have you ever been to Malibu, Lt?" Amanda said while she and Aaron strolled about the old graveyard that hosted no more than two dozen markers, many of them leaning, listing this way and that.

"No, never even been to California," Aaron said, attempting to straighten a stone. Sucessfully bringing the stone upright he said to Amanda, "Find something we can wedge so it will stay." She found a piece of broken tree limb the size of a broom handle and stuck it deep into the crack. "That should work," Aaron said, releasing his grasp on the marker. Amanda noted, again, how powerfully Aaron's upper body was built.

"How did you come up with Malibu for Dr. Porter's office?" Amanda said, brushing her hands together.

"Cool place," Aaron said, "lots of movie stars live there."

"Well, you're starting to let the cat out of the bag, little by little, Aaron ... female DNA in the fish. When do I find out how it got there?"

"Soon, my dear, soon."

Chapter Eight

Burglary was not appropriate protocol for investigative reporting, Jim Streeter mused. Breaking into Dr. Holland's house or car was out of the question. He could rummage through her trash—if he could find it—but he thought that a particularly loathsome violation of privacy.

Her pontoon boat was moored at the dock. Perhaps he could find something there, an unwashed coffee cup or drinking glass. But he couldn't chance stealing even a relatively small item. Given her head of strawberry blonde hair, a strand or two of it might have found its way onto the seat where she sat at the boat's helm. He would have to use the cover of darkness, of course. And a flashlight would be much too risky. He had a lint brush in his duffel, mostly for touching up a suit coat and pants when an interview required coat and tie. He could swab the pontoon's seat where she sat and possibly come up with a bit of hair. She had the dog, of course, no doubt on her lap from time to time while navigating the lake. But the dog wasn't a redhead.

It was well past dusk when Streeter pulled off the side of the gravel road a hundred yards from Josephine Holland's house. A nearly full moon was rising above the treeline across the lake, casting enough light for finding his way along the beach but not so much as to betray his approach and presence on the pontoon. He was going to work quickly—rummaging through nothing on the boat—only passing the lint brush over the seat at the boat's helm then high-tailing it back to his car and returning to Kansas City.

Nearing the dock, he cut to the house and could see two people sitting inside at what looked like a counter in the kitchen. That would be Miss Holland and her friend Kenny Decker whom he had met the day of the fish fry. Where the dog might be, Streeter didn't know. He guessed—hoped—that it was inside; otherwise it would have noted his approach and probably barked by now.

Reaching the dock, Streeter treaded carefully along its gangway. An occasional oak plank squeaked beneath his sneakers, but not enough noise to be heard at the house, he thought. Stepping onto the dock, he moved to the pontoon and swung one leg then the other over its gunnel. The boat rocked slightly beneath his weight. The deck beneath his feet was moist and his sneakers slipped on it once but he caught himself before falling.

Finding the lint brush in his back pocket, he strode the few paces to the boat's helm and passed the brush over the seat several times, especially the upper part where the driver's shoulders would be. He hadn't enough light from the moon to see if the brush had collected what he wanted. Stuffing the brush into his back pocket, he made his way aft to where he had climbed aboard. Swinging a leg onto the dock, he put one foot on the boat's gunnel and was about to jump onto the dock when the wet sole of his sneaker slipped. Losing his balance, he stumbled toward the rear of the boat and went overboard, making a considerable splash when he hit the water. He went under momentarilly but quickly surfaced and grabbed hold of the outboard's lower unit. "Damn!" he blurted, pushing wet hair from his eyes.

Up at the house the dog barked. Streeter heard the door open and voices. He grabbed hold of the pontoon's transom and pulled himself up enough to look toward the house. Josephine and her friend were coming down the deck stairs with a flashlight. The dog was with them. Assuming that they were coming to check on the boat, Streeter eased back into the water. He grasped one of the boat's pontoons and worked his way between the two of them until he was well out of sight when the visitors came onto the dock. Josephine panned the boat with her flashlight. The dog darted about the dock and barked once, having picked up a scent. "Probably a critter," Josephine said while they turned and made their way off the dock.

When Streeter heard the door close at the house, he eased from beneath the boat and pulled his dripping self onto the dock. He felt for the lint brush and found that it was still in his back pocket. Whether or not he had collected a strand of hair, and if his plunge into the lake hadn't washed if free, would have to wait until he got back to his car and some dry clothes. He hoped that near drowning produced something definitive. He sure as hell wasn't going to repeat this. Damn the *particles*. They could go back to where they came from.

Dr. Kaitland Porter opened to UPS and signed for the package. She had gotten a call from Jim Streeter at *The Kansas City Star*. He told of his harrowing experience in falling off Josephine Holland's dock after dark while trying to find a strand of hair—something that could be used in attempting to match DNA. His lint brush had indeed collected a strand or two of hair, two of which belonged to Miss Holland's dog, he suspected. One other, curly and strawberry blonde, belonged to the dog's owner, he believed.

Opening the package, Dr. Porter donned surgical gloves (she hoped Streeter had done the same) and removed the single strand of hair. Holding it between thumb and forefinger, she held it to a light. "Strawberry blonde, alright," she said.

Going to her lab, she prepared chemicals that would expose DNA beneath a microscope. She wondered what of real value this would prove, even if the DNA matched what was found in the fish's vein. That Miss Holland was related to the female whose DNA was found in the fish would leave larger questions—two of them—unanswered: What was the vehicle—or, carrier used to compound the alledged bait? And most importantly, how did the interloping, unidentified particle, mimicking the Higgs boson, perhaps, get into the mix?

Forty years had passed between the prediction of a boson particle *out there* and it actually being found and identified by Peter Higgs of Edinburgh University.

Assuming that the lovely Josephine Holland had built a particle detector of some sort how was she able to capture a boson? Perhaps it found *her*. Her degrees in particle physics and molecular biology would leave one to suspect that she wasn't flying entirely by the seat of her cutoffs. Then again, maybe she was. Young, financially secure, living in a lovely lake house—according to Streeter's account—in America's heartland could find her with plenty of time on her hands for doing what she pleased. If she had been simply trying to keep bordom at bay, by God she had succeeded. She would rock the world of particle physics to its foundations.

Having disclosed DNA in what was presumably a single strand from Miss Holland's head of hair, Dr. Porter attempted to match it with what was found in the fish's vein. She was successful; a positive match. Josephine Holland was definitely related to the female whose DNA had been found in the fish. Whether mother, daughter, sister—or herself couldn't be determined as yet. In this case, at least at this point, it didn't matter. One wasn't trying to solve a murder mystery. If in fact the two catfish Miss Holland brought ashore had morphed into their remarkable size, and I believe they did, Dr. Porter mused while resting back in her chair at the microscope, was it accidental or calculated? She put in a call to Jim Streeter at the *Star*. He wasn't in. She left a message regarding her findings. She herself had no investigating skills beyond her mircoscope. She wondered what Streeter's next move might be.

Jim Streeter sat drinking coffee in the Swinging Bridge Café at Warsaw, Missouri. It was *6:00 a.m.* He had left Kansas City at dusk the evening before. Driving Highway 65 south, he missed his turn at State Road 52 that would have taken him to Gravois Mills where he intended to spend the night. Having found himself in Warsaw instead, he spent the night there rather than double back and risk missing his turn again.

Streeter liked his coffee black; a good thing. The waitress—Dot her name tag said—refreshed his cup with brew so black it looked as though one might be able to seal a parking lot with it. "Fishermen around here like their coffee good and strong," Dot said, seeing Streeter's face blanch while his cup was being topped off.

"Yes, I can see that."

"Keeps 'em from fallin' in the river early of a mornin'," Dot added. Then, "You come to do some fishin'?"

"No, I was headed for Gravois Mills last night but missed my turn."

"Easy to do on these roads after dark," Dot said, turning toward a customer who had just taken a seat in a booth.

Streeter was going to show up at Josephine's Holland's place cold turkey and attempt to get the proverbial cat out of the bag. He knew what she had done, at least in part, and she might as well come clean. He could threathen her with breaking the story, but that wasn't his style. Anyway, the woman wasn't easily intimidated, he suspected. PhDs never are, he considered while testing his coffee once more. They're whip smart and damn well know it. Add Josephine Holland's red hair to it and you might have a bitch on wheels if you get her ire up. He wished that he had Dr. Porter with him. He was on his own and he could only relate her findings. Fortunately she had kept it simple: human DNA in the fish; female; matches Miss Holland's. The ball would be in her court. He had one opening question for her and it would be direct: What were you trying to do, Dr. Holland?

Streeter reached Josephine Holland's house at mid-morning. There was no need, this trip, to conceal his car and approach on foot. He noted that the pontoon was at its mooring, an indication that the subject of his visit was home. A newish looking Chevy Tahoe was parked beneath a carport next to a BMW. He suspected that the SUV belonged to her friend Kenny Decker. It was early fall now and foliage among the densely wooded hills was yellowing. A pair of redbud trees near the carport were losing their leaves, most of which had blown into the carport.

Bringing his car to a stop behind the Tahoe, Streeter exited and began making his was to the stairs that led to the home's deck. Given the proximity of the vehicles, he supposed that the deck intrance was used most of the time. He heard the dog bark as he began to ascend the stairs. Josephine slid the door open. "Well, Mr. Streeter, to what do I owe this pleasant surprize?" Streeter only smiled as he neared the entrance. "Have you had breakfast?" Josephine added, ushering her guest inside.

"Yes, but a little coffee would be good, though."

Moving on into the main living area that openly joined the kitchen, Streeter greeted Kenny Decker and the two men exchanged handshakes. Decker had a faint but knowing smile working at the corners of his mouth. He and Josephine cast looks at each other. Ellie, who was to clean this day, was sitting at the bar and finishing a slice of toast. Sodipop needed some recognition from the visitor and Streeter reached down and patted the dog's head.

Accepting his coffee, Streeter took a seat next to Ellie. He tested the brew with satisfaction, noting its contrast with that of the Swinging Bridge Café from which he still felt wired.

Silence had grown palpable. Ellie coughed and said she had such a tickle in her throat. Josephine suggested a drink of water.

May I cut to the chase?" Streeter said at last.

"Please do," Josephine said. "You're a reporter for the *Star*, Mr. Streeter. I doubt that you've driven all the way from Kansas City just to say hello and have a cup of coffee."

"When I was here for your fish fry back in the summer," Streeter began, "I was impressed, to say the least, with the photos of those two monster catfish."

"Yes, they were remarkable," Josephine said. Decker nodded in agreement.

"Very fine eating, too, I might add. Actually, I took a piece of it home with me, not to eat, however. I packed it in dry ice and sent it to Dr. Kaitland Porter at the California Institute of Metamorphic Biology."

"May I ask why?" Josephine said, picking up her coffee cup and swirling the contents slowly.

"I had a hard time swallowing the worms."

Ellie giggled.

"No pun intented," Streeter added.

"And what did your Dr. Porter find?" Josephine asked, persuing with something between amusement and intrigue rising in her expression. Kenny fetched the coffee pot and refreshed cups.

"Nothing at first," Streeter said.

"At first?" Josephine said with tongue in cheek.

"Upon further examination, disecting a bit deeper into the specimen of fish, one of its veins, to be precise, she found DNA."

"Fish have DNA," Mr. Streeter.

"Please call me Jim." Josephine nodded.

"Indeed they do. But the DNA Dr. Porter found was human—female."

"So we're talking mermaid here," Josephine said.

"Not quite. I have a confession to make. I took the liberty of snooping about your pontoon one night in search of a strand of your lovely hair so that DNA could be extracted by Dr. Porter."

"You're lucky that you weren't shot," Josephine said.

"I fell from your boat and nearly drowned."

"It would have served you right."

"Dr. Porter got a positive match. You and the female DNA in the fish are related.

"My mother," Josephine said, knowing that the gig was up, more or less.

"What were you trying to do?" Streeter asked.

"As you probably know, Mr—Jim, I have doctorates in particle physics and molecular biology. I also have more money and time than I know what to do with much of the time. So, to pass a little time and spend a few bucks, I built a miniture particle detector. I named it Lazarus. I put a tablespoon each of my mother and father's cremated remains in it and hit the switch."

Ellie gasped and put a hand over her mouth. Kenny turned to Josephine as his jaw came slowly ajar.

Josephine shifted a bit on her stool as she turned her attention to Kenny then alternating between the others. "When we were pulling weeds at the cemetery do you remember me telling you that mom and dad weren't buried there?"

"I do remember," Kenny said.

"You probably wondered why they hadn't asked to be buried there, being so fond of the little graveyard, mowing, pulling weeds."

"I did wonder," Kenny said.

"Well, mom and dad were avid fishermen and they loved the lake. Mom always said that she and dad wanted to be cremated. She thought that gravesites, markers and all that were just something to make people feel guilty about not visiting very often, only on Memorial Day, maybe … they used to call it Decoration Day."

"Some still do," Streeter said, taking up his coffee cup and feeling his pulse racing with this unfolding revelation.

"Anyway," Josephine continued, "mom wanted their remains cast into the lake that they so loved. But I thought that was so sudden, you know, over too soon, like—well ... So I got this crazy idea about using their remains in a different way. I wanted to make some bait out of some of it, but I couldn't get it to stick together. Finally, I wondered what would happen if I put a little of the remains in the detector and see what Lazarus might do."

"So what happened?" Streeter said.

"I hit the switch and when the thing quit humming I opened the door and there sat two tidy little cubes of mom and dad's remains."

"Would your parents have objected to you using them as fish bait?" Streeter said, tipping his head slightly. A smile played at the corners of his mouth.

Josephine laughed and said, "You make me sound awful."

"I think it's cool," Ellie said.

"Anyway, I tied one of the cubes on a fishing line— I couldn't get a hook into it--and cast it into the lake, just off the dock."

"What happened?" Streeter said.

"Nothing."

"I went back to to the drawing board," Josephine continued. "What if I extract some DNA from something of moms and introduce it into her cube? I found a curl of her baby hair in a locket. I extracted DNA and poured it onto the cube and went fishing again off the dock. A twenty-pound channelcat grabbed it and wouldn't turn loose while I reeled it in."

"Jesus!" Streeter mumbled

"Anyway, I found DNA on dad's favorite pipe, extracted it and poured it onto his cube." Josephine paused for a moment and took a drink from her coffee cup. "Kenny and I went fishing, this time up to Palisades bluffs and deep water. I tied both of the cubes on a half inch line and Kenny threw them into the water."

"Hense the two monster catfish?" Streeter said.

"Yes. They slammed the pontoon into the bluff a couple of times. I put the boat in reverse, full throttle, and managed to pull us away. Our catch began towing us home. About halfway there they surfaced for a short time. Kenny and I could hardly believe our eyes. When we got home and put a bullet into each of their heads and weighed them, one was 300 pounds; the other 325 pounds, actually," Josephine said. "Kenny is a mechanical engineer and he saw a wire inside the detector that I hadn't connected. No need for it, I thought. We connected it, put mom and dad's cubes back inside the detector. A message began to crawl across my computer screen telling me that I had altered circuitry and was about to circumvent—not violate, it said—certain laws of physics and biology, and did I want to continue. I was a little afraid to go ahead but Kenny and Ellie convinced me to go for it. When the detector finished doing its thing, we opened the door and found that mom and dad's cubes had been joined."

"Very clever," Streeter said.

"I thought so," Josephine said. "Mom and dad were married for 53 years."

"Have you gone fishing with the new cube?" Streeter asked.

"No."

"Why not?"

"I'm afraid to."

"Why?"

"Those two monster catfish caused quite a stir around the lake ... brought a reporter to my door. "God only knows what might happen if I pitch that altered cube into the water. I could have half the world at my doorstep. I value my privacy."

"Dr. Porter thinks that what you've done has somehow caused the fish to morph into their remarkable size," Streeter said.

"I agree," Josephine said.

"Would you have any objections to meeting with Dr. Porter?" Streeter said

"I really wouldn't care to travel to California right now."

"I think that she would be happy to travel here," Streeter said.

Jim Streeter was waiting for Dr. Porter's plane to land at Springfield National Airport. It was mid-morning on a Saturday. He was standing with a cardboard sign that read: Dr. Kaitland Porter? Disembarking passengers began streaming into the terminal. Streeter searched their faces. One female noted him and his sign and smiled, quickening her pace toward him. She reached into a front pocket of her tweed slacks and found a dollar bill. Upon reaching Streeter she handed the bill to him. He laughed and said, "Thank you, mam."

"We've got a panhandler on about every corner in LA," Dr. Porter said.

"I kind of felt like one," Streeter said, chuckling as the two of them turned and began making their way from the terminal.

"How far is it to Miss Holland's place?" Dr. Porter said as they neared Streeter's car.

"About an hour and a half."

During their drive to the lake Streeter told Dr. Porter what Josephine had used for the fish bait.

"You're kidding," Dr. Porter said, her jaw dropping.

"I was as shocked as you," Streeter said.

Streeter and Dr. Porter reached the lake and Josephine's house just before noon. Making their way up the steps, they were soon greeted by Kenny Decker who slid the glass door open for them. Josephine appeared beside him. Introductions were made, including Ellie who had been cleaning this day.

Streeter had cued Josephine regarding when he thought they would arrive. Lunch was being prepared and she thought that baking some of the fish would be appropriate, seeing that it was pretty much the subject of this visit. The guests found seats at the kitchen's bar and Josephine served coffee and said that lunch was almost ready. She opened an oven door and checked the fish. Turning to Dr. Porter she said, "Baked catfish okay?"

"Certainly, and it smells wonderful."

Ellie finished some dusting she was doing on the home's second floor then came downstairs when lunch was announced. Dr. Porter sampled her fish and commented on how delicious it was. "I don't need to tell you what a remarkable development this is," she said, looking to Josephine. "I'm curious as to what you were attempting to do."

"I really wasn't trying to *do* anything," Josephine said, "just a silly idea that came into my head."

"Days can get a little long on the lake sometimes," Kenny said.

"Have you gone fishing again?" Dr. Porter asked, having a drink of sweet iced tea."

"No, and I'm afraid too," Josephine said, laughing softly.

"Why?"

"There's—uh, been a strange development."

Kenny nodded and smiled at Ellie who was quietly enjoying her lunch though she was clearly listening to the conversation.

"What sort of development?" Dr. Porter said, forking a bit of coleslaw.

"Kenny noted a wire that I had left unattached in the detector. I saw no use for it. He and Ellie thought I should connect it. So I did. Computer read out told me that cirquitry had be altered and that I would have to re-program."

"What happened?" Dr. Porter asked.

"I put mom and dad's cubes back in the detector and hit the switch."

Jim Streeter chuckled.

"The familiar green glow began to appear," Josephine continued, "then it turned to purple, then red, back to green again and shut down. Kenny tried to open the detector's door but it wouldn't open. He looked through the glass and saw only a single cube."

"Interesting," Dr. Porter said. "What do you think happened?"

"Mom and dad were married 53 years. Soldering that last wire into place joined them again, somehow. Purple was mom's favorite color; dad liked red."

"The particle I saw somewhat resembled the Higgs boson," Dr. Porter said, "but you may have captured something else, a yet unidentified particle."

"Whatever it is, it appears to have a sense of humor," Josephine said.

"Yes, and a mind of its own," Kenny said.

Josephine had baked quite a batch of fish. After lunch—blackberry cobbler for dessert—she asked her guests if they would like to take a cruise on her pontoon. They would go down to Palisades' bluffs where the two fish were caught, then pay a visit on Evelyn at the church. Josephine wanted to take her some fish and an extra cobbler she had baked.

When all were aboard the pontoon, Josephine backed the boat away from the dock and set a course down lake. She opened the outboard to three-quarter throttle and arrived at the bluffs in less than thirty minutes. She brought the pontoon alongside the towering bluff, staying out twenty feet or so, and easing along slowly so that her guests could marvel at the great wall of limestone. Cruising in closer, she pointed out the ring in the rock where she and Kenny had tied up when casting their line into the water. Scrapes were visible in the limestone where the two fish had slammed the pontoon into the wall before Kenny untied the boat and Josephine put the Merc in hard reverse.

Leaving the Palisades and a five minute cruise back up lake, Josephine nosed the pontoon ashore where the party would disembark and take the trail that led to the cemetery and old church. Dr. Porter and Jim Streeter wanted to have a look at the pre-Civil War graveyard. Sodipop led the way, looking back often to see if all were following.

After strolling about the cemetery for a few minutes, the party walked the short distance to the church where they hoped to find Evelyn at home. She was indeed and happily ushered her guests inside. She had been working on a quilt and the rack upon which it was stretched was stationed near what had once been the church's chancel. Dr. Porter was particularly taken by the quilt. "It's just lovely," she said while running one hand over a section of the design. Evelyn said that she would probably have it finished by Thanksgiving. She was going to give it to a granddaughter for her hope chest. Since the church was no longer used for worship services, a private home now, all but two of the pews had been removed. After Evelyn's son purchased the church for his mother, in addition to having a proper bathroom built, as well as central heat and air conditioning, he carpeted the church in a plush, forest green, his mother's favorite color.

Evelyn had a fresh pitcher of tea and she served her

guests. Josephine presented her with the freshly baked catfish—quite a platter of it—and cobbler. During the course of conversation, Josephine asked Evelyn if she had seen Marvin lately. She said no, not for while, but when the wind was right she could hear his banjo. And she thought that he must have found a friend for his music was often accompanied by fiddle of late. Quite entertaining, Evelyn said, sampling a piece of the fish with her fingers. She said, too, that since Josephine had brought more fish than she could possibly eat, she would like to take some of it, a little of the cobbler as well, to Marvin. "He's just a rack of bones," Evelyn said. "I wonder if he gets enough to eat half the time. There's not much meat on a squirrel, and work at the saw mill is slow right now, I've heard. He plays his banjo around the lake some at one place or another, but it doesn't pay much. He does it mostly for fun and something to eat. He visits the food pantry in Camdenton sometimes when things get really bad. He's awfully independent and proud. I had to talk him into it. I said there's no shame."

"Certainly not," Dr. Porter said. Jim Streeter concurred.

"It's such a lovely day. It'll be a nice walk through the woods to Marvin's place," Josephine said. Everybody agreed.

Evelyn seperated some of the fish, half of the cobbler as well and the party set out through the forest to Marvin's. They had walked for a couple hundred yards when Evelyn brought them to a stop and said, "Well, here we are."

"Where's his house?" Dr. Porter said. Josephine and Ellie were smiling.

"Up there," Evelyn said, casting her eyes into the branches of a great white oak that held in its embrace a two storied treehouse of remarkable construction. It had a pitched roof with cedar shakes. The sides of the tree house were cedar shakes as well. On the lower story a porch rested on enormous limbs as big around as an elephant's leg. Two cane chairs were stationed on either side of a rough hewn door that let into the home, though one would have to more or less crawl through the opening. The treehouse was heated in winter by a lightweight propane stove that could easily be carried from one level to the other. Nailed to the trunk of the tree five feet up from the ground was a homemade plaque which read: "Yea verily I say unto thee except a man live in a tree he cannot be." The tree and its lofty house sat on five acres willed to Marvin by a favorite uncle.

Everybody chuckled at the sign's wording then Evelyn called out, "Marvin, are you home?"

"Yes mam," Marvin returned, opening the treehouse's door and sticking his head out. He crawled out onto the porch. He was wearing bib overalls. Close on his heels was a female. She was short and round. She had a cherub face with large blue eyes. Her hair was flaxen and pulled back into a ponytail. She was wearing denim cutoffs and a yellow print tee shirt that demonstrated ample breasts—braless, it would appear—and they never seemed to quit moving entirely. Coming alongside Marvin, she smiled and waved at those down below.

"We brought you some freshly baked catfish and blackberry cobble, Marvin," Evelyn said.

"Yummee," Marvin returned.

"There's a condition, though," Josephine put in.

"And what would that be dear Josephine?" Marvin introduced his friend as   Mae.

"You must play us a tune on your banjo," Josephine said.

"If Mae accompanies me on her fiddle, can she have some fish and cobbler too?" Marvin said.

"Certainly."

Marvin and Mae disappeared into the house for a moment then returned with their respective instruments in hand. They took seats on the cane chairs on either side of the door. "What would you like to hear?" Marvin said.

"Anything at all," Evelyn ventured.

The two musicians conferred in soft tones, checked their instrument's tuning, then Mae drew the bow across the strings of her fiddle and produced the sound of a train's whistle. She plucked the strings a coupel of times that sounded like a bell then broke into *Orange Blossom Special* to the applause of those standing below. Marvin picked up the pace with his banjo.

"My God! They're wonderful," Dr. Porter said.

So excited had Josephine become that she took Kenny by his hands and began to dance in a circle with him. Ellie did the same with Streeter then turned him loose and motioned for him to give Dr. Porter a whirl, which he did.

The tune, lasting about three minutes, came to a

close. Those down below, breathless now, applauded wildly. Then, "Can the two of you come down and get the fish and cobbler, Marvin?" Evelyn said. Marvin nodded and threw down a rope ladder. Mae descended first followed by Marvin. When the two of them were on ground level they shook hands all around. Marvin said that he had met Mae at the food pantry in Camdenton.

"I was traveling with a bluegrass band and it broke up. I'd been living in my car and it went kaput," Mae said. "I couldn't afford to fix it. So I just junked it. I met Marvin at the pantry, we started talking and he said that I could come and stay with him. We had to walk here." She laughed and took Marvin by an arm.

"What did you think of his treehouse?" Evelyn said.

"Awsome!

The group chatted for a short while longer then Dr. Porter withdrew a fifty dollar bill from her purse and gave it to the couple. "Thank you for the wonderful entertainment," she said. Marvin and Mae thanked her profusely. Goodbyes were said. Marvin ascended the treehouse's rope ladder then let down a basket. Mae put the fish and cobble in the basket and Marvin hoisted it aloft. She took to the rope ladder and she and Marvin sat on their porch and enjoyed what had been given to them.

After escorting Evelyn back to the church, the party returned to the pontoon and headed back up lake for Gravois Mills. On the way, Dr. Porter asked if she might have a look at the detector and a demonstration. Josephine agreed.

"So now we know," Amanda said while reading the first draft of what Aaron had written. "You're a *sick* individual, Lt.," she said jokingly. "Creamated remains for fish bait!"

"Hey, it's what she wanted—sort of—Josephine's mother," Aaron said.

"Could this really happen?"

"Of course, we're making it happen. Anyway, we're having fun writing it, aren't we? That's some treehouse," Aaron added.

"My sisters and I had a treehouse in our backyard when I was growing up in Des Moines, not as big as Marvin's, of course."

"Marvin's girlfriend ... buxum," Aaron said.

"Most guys like big boobs. I'm taking the next chapter, Lt, part of it, anyway," Amanda said. "Walking around in the old graveyard gave me some ideas. I wonder how long it's been since a new grave was dug here?"

"Ages, I'd say."

Chapter Nine

Vernon Vault, president of the Amalgamated, Fede-
rarted Funeral Director's Association of America LLC
(AFFDA0ALLC) sat at his desk and pored over a troub-
ling bit of data coming in from America's heartland,
central Missouri, specifically. Funeral Directors in certain counties, curiously surrounding Missouri's massive
Lake of the Ozarks, were reporting a sharp drop in traditional services. Lucrative casket sales were virtually
coming to a standstill. Not so much as one hole had
been dug in a cemetery for months, though death notic-
es were more than steady, given the aging of popula-
tions. "What the hell is going on down there?" Vernon
mumbled, turning a page on the spreadsheet before
him. A number of funeral homes were near filing for
bankruptcy, for their storeroom of caskets, ranging from
$2,000 for a basic box to $10,000 for mohogany,
bronze, and copper, were not moving. No funeral home
could survive on a paltry 500 bucks or so for creamation
services—even if they had a crematory on site—and
that was about all the requests they were getting of late.

Ornate urns for ashes were not selling; mourners were bringing their own cardboard boxes for loved one's remains. Vernon decided that it was time to send an investigator to the Show-Me state before every funeral home without a crematorium went belly up. He himself would do the investigating. He asked his secretary to book him a flight to Kansas City and reserve a car for his trip deep into the Missouri Ozarks.

Shortly after Jim Streeter's attendance at Josephine Holland's fish fry and his subsequent correspondence with Dr. Porter, he had developed a theory regarding the *carrier* in which the mysterious sub-atomic particle as well as DNA from Miss Holland's mother was riding. Every theory must have a prediction, however, and Streeter had been ready to make one, partly prompted by an article he read by the *Associated Press* regarding what was becoming something of a freefall in traditional funeral services in Missouri, especially its central part. Hords of grievers were opting for cremation, leaving funeral directors holding the bag on caskets that virtually no visitor would so much as view. What's more, lovely urns were gathering dust while family members brought along cardboard boxes for depositing remains. Pushing urns, even putting them on sale, impressed no mourners ... mourners? Actually, funeral home directors spoke of the contrary: folks were rather jubilant. "I've come for mom," said one woman, smiling widely while clutching her cardboard box to her breast and practically skipping across the funeral home's lobby.

Streeter's theory turned out to be correct, for he learned, directly from Miss Holland herself, that what she had used as a carrier for the sub-atomic particle and her mother's DNA was in fact her own mother's cremated remains. Her father's remains had been used as well; his DNA presumably introduced to the substance. And at some point after the fish fry, somebody had the same notion and leaked it, not to the press or the Internet, but to a neighbor, then another, then another until half the folks in central Missouri were contriving ways to do what Miss Holland had done. Streeter suspected that the young girl, Ellie, Josephine Holland's house cleaner, had leaked the info, though not necessarily on purpose.

There were increasing incidents of mircowave ovens catching on fire. Nobody had been hurt or homes burned to the ground—yet, though there were reports of some microwaves blasting through a home's waterfront window or wall and landing in the lake. These incidents were based on a common misunderstanding of what Josephine was using to produce the cubes that caught the two outlandishly large catfish. Somebody had learned that the detector looked like a microwave oven. The error, of course, was that it wasn't simply a microwave. The uninitiated were placing loved one's cremated remains—many freshly fetched in their cardboard box from a crematorium—far too much of them into a mircowave, presumably for good measure, tossing in a strand of hair, piece of a garment that might contain DNA, and hitting the switch in hopes of producing what

Miss Holland created for catching the remarkable fish; entrepreneurial notions among some fantazied about selling great amounts of catfish on the market.

One preacher back in the hills envisioned feeding the world. When experimenting with his late wife's cremated remains, the microwave in the church's basement became a missile, of sorts, and blasted through the basement ceiling, the sanctuary ceiling as well, and blew the steeple off of the pastor's little house of worship.

Should these psuedo scientists learn that Josephine's machine was specially wired to detect sub-atomic particles—one now that appeared to be mimicking the Higgs boson—and manage to duplicate its construction, there was no hope that they could achieve the same results for they hadn't the physics equation, which lay in Josephine Holland's pretty head, for activating the device. At any rate, something had to be done to stop these insane attempts to create what Miss Holland had before tradedy struck and somebody set fire to the entire Ozarks mountain range.

Josephine and Kenny became alarmingly aware of what was going on around them and spreading rapidly across central Missouri, the most intense activity being in the general vacinity of the lake. Curiously enough, it wasn't locals, for the most part, who were engaging in these experiments. They had more common sense. Rather it was out-of-towners, visiting their lake houses on weekends mostly, who were doing it. There was little doubt that what was taking place on the top floor of Miss Holland's house had been leaked. That doubt was erased when Ellie showed up unanouced with her younger sister, Alice, in tow. Both girls were teary-eyed when Ellie spoke: "Miss Holland, I never told you that I talk in my sleep a lot."

"Oh, God," Josephine whispered to herself, casting a look at Kenny.

"One night, when I was talking in my sleep it woke Alice up and she heard me talking about what you did with your mom and dad's cremated remains and how they caught the big fish."

Alice eased closer to her sister and snuffed back tears.

Ellie continued: "Alice didn't know about my promise not to tell and she told some kids at school. I'm so sorry, Miss Holland," Ellie said then bursting into tears. Her sister began to weep as well.

"It's ok, girls," Josephine said, pulling the sisters to her. "It was only a matter of time before this all got out," Josephine added, releasing the girls.

"Am I fired from my job?" Ellie asked.

"Of course not, sweetheart. I could never replace you," Josephine said, pulling the girl to her once more.

Josephine insisted on the girls staying for lunch. And it was a much happier scene. They talked about what people were doing with their microwave ovens. "It's so crazy!" Ellie said. "What are you going to do, Miss Holland?"

"Nothing for now. I'm sure that our *Kansas City Star* reporter will break this story soon. I'll just deal with it as it comes."

Vernon Vault, president of the Amalgamated, Federated Funeral Director's Association of America LLC (AFF-DAOALLC) exited highway 52 at Cole Camp, Missouri and parked in front of a small café. He needed some lunch and a cup of coffee and time to get his thoughts together regarding where his investigation should begin. His map told him that he wasn't far from Gravois Mills where Josephine Holland lived. She was the source of the problem which he had come to look into.

Inside the café he ordered chichen friend steak and coffee. The waitress, Madge, her name tag said, was talkative enough; the lunch crowd hadn't begun to arrive. Sampling his coffee and taking a knife and fork to the meat on his plate, he said while Madge was still near, "I'm doing a story (he lied) on how Funeral Homes are doing in the Ozarks."

"Some of them are about to close their doors," Madge said, taking up a towel and wiping a stain on the counter.

"What's the problem?" Vernon said after chewing a bite of steak and sampling his coffee.

"Everybody's goin' for cremation all of a sudden around here. Funeral homes ain't makin' much ... got to sell them expensive caskets."

"Interesting," Vernon said, gazing at Madge over the rim of his coffee cup.

"There's somethin' else," Madge said, refreshing Vernon's cup. "Folks have been puttin' their loved ones ashes in mircowaves and blowin' the hell out of things." She laughed and set the coffee pot back on its warmer.

"Why?" Vernon said, feeling his pulse begin to

quicken.

"Josephine Holland—gal who lives down at Gravois Mills—made some sort of thingamajig that makes special fish bait. Word spread around that she used her mom and dad's ashes to make the stuff. People say she's plumb scary smart, got PhDs up the yang yang."

"What's the thing look like?" Vernon said.

"I haven't seen it, but people who have say it looks kind of like a large mircrowave."

Bingo! Vernon thought while setting his coffee cup down.

"It ain't no microwave at all," Madge said, "just looks like one. People jumped to conclusions, like they do, and thought they could do what Miss Holland did. A preacher back in the hills put a bunch of his late wife's ashes in a mircowave. The damn thing took off like a rocket, went through the basement ceiling and blew the steeple off the church."

"Good Lord!"

"Good Lord is right," Madge said. "I don't think Jesus would appreciate that little church being hurt like that."

"I'd like to talk to the pastor," Vernon said. "Can you tell me how to get to the church?"

Madge drew Vernon a map to the church, a nearby funeral home as well, which he requested. He paid his bill and returned to his car. He'd call on the funeral director first then try and locate the pastor. Having a talk with Josephine Holland would be his next stop.

The Shady Grove Funeral Home was a short distance down the road from Cole Camp. An older black Fleetwood hearse sat out front. One of its front tires was flat and looked to have been so for a while, for grass had grown rather high upon the wheel. No other vehicles were present. The older hearses, especially the black ones, gave Vernon the hebeejeebees. It had been many years since he worked as an undertaker. An attorney prepared a living will for Vernon. He explicitly stated that he was to be carted to the graveyard in anything other than a black hearse. He thought cremation distastful.

Vernon found the front door unlocked. Sticking his head inside, he called out rather softly in curious reverence, as though he feared waking the dead. No response. He ventured on into the lobby. Not caring to call out again, he strode down a hallway toward a door that was slightly ajar. Peeking inside, he saw a grey haired man sitting at a desk. He was spooning pork 'n beans from a can. An opened box of saltines sat on his desk. One of the wafers was between his thumb and forefinger. Half of the cracker had been bitten off. The old man dipped the remaining half into the bean juice then plopped it into his mouth. He turned in his chair when Vernon spoke: "Hello."

The old fellow set the can of beans down on his desk, wiped his mouth rather shakingly with the back of his hand, like a drunk needing a drink, and said, "If you're inquiring into creamation for a loved one—or yourself, I don't have a crematory. You'll have to go elsewhere."

Vernon introduced himself as president of AFF-

DAOALLC. The older man, having been a funeral director for fifty years, was a member of the Association. He rose and shook hands with his visitor then motioned for him to have a seat. "How can I help you?" he said when Vernon was seated. "I would offer you some lunch, but as you can see—he pointed to the can of beans—I've fallen on rather hard times."

Vernon nodded then said, "Yes I can see that."

Without letting Vernon launch into the purpose of his visit, the old man said, "It's that goddamn Josephine Holland down to Gravois Mills who has caused this!"

"Yes, I understand that she's involved."

"*Involved* is an understatement," the old man said, pushing the can of beans a few inches across his desk, as though it might give him some breathing room. "I used to like her—especially the big fish fry she has for everbody each summer—but I had no idea that those humongous catfish would be the ruination of my business."

"What did she catch them on?" Vernon asked, though he knew from his talk with Madge at the café in Cole Camp.

"Did something to her mother and father's cremated remains, turned them into fish bait." He laughed encredulously and shook his head. "Hell of a way to treat your folks, turn 'em into a piece of damn bait!"

"Interprizing woman," Vernon said.

"Maybe so, but I wish to hell she'd done her interprizing somewhere else. I haven't sold a coffin for three months. My grave digger is on food stamps. I'll apply for mine on Monday, I guess. I got to have something to eat besides these—he motioned toward the half eaten can of beans—or I'll turn this office into a jet propulsion laboratory. I suppose that redheaded hellion at Gravois Mills would like that." He picked up a tube of the crackers and offered them to his guest, who declined.

"Well, maybe things will get better," Vernon said.

"Not anytime soon. Folks around the hills are blowin' these Ozarks half way to kingdom come, Microwaves shootin' through walls, windows, roofs, trying to do what Josephine did. I guess they'll give up when they run out of ashes, and that ain't likely to happen with the way old folks keep dying off. By God I haven't seen a cadaver for months. Outfit picked up the last of my coffins a few days ago … couldn't pay for them. I guess if somebody shows up wantin' to bury a loved one proper like, I'll have to make them a pine box."

"I'm down here looking into things," Vernon said. "I don't know what I can do, other than see if what she's doing is legal."

"Hell, she ain't doing *nothin'* now," the old man said. "It's the morons trying to do what she did. I hope to God nobody gets their hands on that contraption she made. I suspect, though, that how to run the damn thing is in her head. They'd play hell gettin' that from a redhead."

"You dislike readheads?" Vernon said.

"I love 'em, just temperamental as all get-out. I had a redheaded girlfriend once. I pissed her off and she cranked me upside the head with a fryin' pan. Liked to killed me. I ain't right yet."

Vernon chuckled then bid the old fellow goodbye

and returned to his car. He consulted the map Madge had drawn for him then set out through the hills for Beulah Land Community Church, which Madge had noted on the top of the map. You can't miss it, she had said, sits among a stand of red cedar.

Beulah Land Community Church sat on a knoll among a dozen large red cedars. They swayed gently under a crisp breeze coming out of the northwest this early October day. Vernon picked up their acrid scent when exiting his car. The church was typical of what is sometimes called "open country" churches: one room, usually accomodating a maximum of 60 or 70 worshipers, though rarely rising above 40 or so on any given Sunday with the exception of Easter and Christmas.

Vernon strode toward the church's front door. He noted an extention ladder leaning against the south wall of the building. It appeared that someone had been working on the gash in the roof where a steeple had been blown away by the trajectory of the mircowave. Vernon clucked his tongue and shook is head in wonderment, amazed that the church hadn't burned to the ground. Mounting a flight of six steps, the visitor found the front door unlocked. No need to knock when entering a church, he thought as he opened the door and stepped into a small foyer. A picture of Jesus hung on one wall. Coat hooks, a dozen of them, ran on either side of the picture. A table with one drawer and an opened guest book sat near the door. Swinging doors opened into the sanctuary. Vernon peeked inside. A man was sitting on a front pew nearest the chancel and pulpit. He was quite still. Vernon thought that he might be praying. He eased back out of the church and sat on the steps, waiting to hear movement inside.

He hadn't waited long when he heard the swinging door inside the foyer being opened. Shortly a man exited the church. "Good afternoon," the fellow said.

"Hello," Vernon returned, coming to his feet.

"I'm Pastor Rainwater," the man said, extending a hand. "How can I help you?" The man looked to be in his early sixties. He was dressed in work clothes, splotches of white paint were on the legs of khaki pants and a blue sweatshirt. He had a full head of dark hair, greying mostly around the temples. His eyes were dark as nuggets of coal. He was a handsome fellow and his voice was a rich baratone, suitable for proclaiming the gospel.

Vernon decided not to reveal his professional credentials. "I'm a freelance writer," he began "and I'm interested in the microwave problems folks have been having around here."

"*Problems* alright," the pastor said. "Mine went through the basement ceiling, sanctuary ceiling and blew steeple off the church."

"I noted the damage to the roof when I drove up," Vernon said. "Where's the steeple now?" he added.

"Bottom of the lake, probably, along with the microwave."

"Any idea what caused it?"

The pastor shifted his weight awkwardly then suggested that the two of them have a seat on the steps. "I'll tell you what I think, but I don't want my name or the church's name put in any newspaper ... embarrassing, what I did. I come near gettin' my walkin' papers over it."

"I understand."

"There's this woman over to Gravois Mills," the pastor began, "Josephine Holland, scientist, I guess, who came up with a way to make fish bait that can catch huge catfish. She landed two 300 pound bluecats last summer."

"What did she use?" Vernon asked, though he already knew. He wanted to see if the pastor's explanation was the same.

"She took some of her mother and father's cremated remains, added their DNA to it, and put 'em in a machine that folks say looks like a microwave. She must have done something to it, though. I put a bunch of Ann's ashes—that's my late wife—and a strand of her hair I got from one of her hair brushes. The hair was supposed to add the needed DNA. Sweet Sheppard of Judea! It added *something*! The thing took off like a Saturn rocket. I come near crapin' in my pants."

Vernon suppressed an urge to laugh, for the pastor was as sober as an AA member sitting at a meeting.

The pastor passed a hand across his brow then continued: "At first I thought that God—or, Ann was trying to tell me something. But when I heard that this was happening all over the place, especially around the lake, I didn't take it so personal."

"Is it still going on?" Vernon said.

"Yes. Word spread that what Miss Holland was using to make the bait wasn't a mircowave afterall, just looked like one. Well, you know how bullheaded people can be. Some are thinking that they can rig one up like she did and get the same affect. They're gettin' the same affect alright, sending those microwaves through the ceiling and walls! It's a wonder nobody's been killed."

"Why did you try it?" Vernon asked.

"I'm a minister and I care about people, especially hungry ones. Fish the size or bigger than the ones Miss Holland caught could feed a lot of hungry folks, and I'd give it to 'em free. Just bring your knives and ice chests and have at it."

"Can't blame you for that."

"What puzzles me most," the pastor continued, "is why the things had to take off like they did, tear stuff up and all?"

"It's weird, like something made them mad," Vernon said.

The two men sat silently for long moments then Vernon rose and said goodbye. He had one more stop to make. He would get things from the proverbial horse's mouth this time. Providing that he didn't get lost, he should make it to Josephine Holland's place a little before dark.

"I thought *I* was going off the deep end," Aaron said, toweling himself after a bath in the lake. He could scarcely get his eyes off Amanda's glistening breasts as she waded from the water and bent to pick up her towel. "That's the wildest thing I ever heard, Microwave ovens blasting through ceilings and walls."

"Keeping pace with you, Lt. wasn't easy. I had to come up with something big."

"People who knew the film director, Cecil B. De-Mille said that he would bite off more than he could chew then chewed it," Aaron said, drawing on a pair of undershorts. "We may end up having to do the same thing."

"So, what's next?" Amanda said, pulling on clean panties and tee shirt.

"Don't know just yet. Maybe they should go fishing again."

"A bigger fish?"

"We'll see."

"You know what's starting to worry me?" Amanda said.

"What's that?" Aaron said as he and Amanda headed for the tent.

"How are we going to end this thing?"

"E.L. Doctorow said something to the effect that writing a novel is like driving cross-country at night. You can only go as far as your headlights will let you. But it can be done."

"I just hope our lights don't go out," Amanda said, "or we might just end up in the middle of a desert with no way out."

"We've come this far, girl. I think we can do it."

Chapter Ten

The sun was just beginning to set when Vernon Vault pulled into the drive at Josephine Holland's place. Given the arrangement of the driveway it appeared that the usual entrance was at a sliding glass door on the home's deck that looked out onto the lake. Vernon mounted the steps and knocked on the door. Josephine opened to him. Sodipop was at her side, his curly cue tail switching, always ready to welcome a visitor.

Inside, Vernon introduced himself and his AFF-DAOALLC credentials which drew curious looks from those in the room. He was introduced to Kenny Decker and Jim Streeter of *The Kansas City Star*. Cocktails were being taken and Vernon had a scotch and water. Everybody was sitting at the kitchen bar and Vernon found a stool there as well. After a few pleasantries, he went immediately to the subject of this visit: "Data has been coming steadily into my office regarding what seems to be a freefall in coffin sales in the central part of this state. Droves of folks are suddenly opting for cremation at a rate never seen before in our industry."

Josephine passed a hand across her forehead and shot a look at Kenny and Jim Streeter.

Vernon noted the body language, sampled his drink then continued: "Though the remarkable shift from traditional burial to cremation is restricted, for the time being, to central Missouri, especially around your Lake of the Ozarks, it has all but bankrupted many funeral directors who depend on coffin sales, vaults, and preparing grave sites. Earlier today I visited a funeral director near Cole Camp. The poor fellow was eating pork 'n beans from a can. It was quite sad. He's going to apply for food stamps on Monday."

This drew guarded smiles from those in the room.

Vernon ignored the response and continued: "Earlier today I visited with Pastor Rainwater at his Beulah Land Community Church. He attempted to reproduce what you've done, Miss Holland, in creating fish bait for attracting very large fish, catfish in particular. His microwave—the church's, perhaps I should say—launched and blasted through the basement ceiling, into the sanctuary and out the roof, taking with it the steeple."

"My God!" Josephine said, putting a hand over her mouth. Kenny and Jim Streeter clucked their tongues and shook their heads.

"I'd like very much to see the devise that you've built, Miss Holland," Vernon said.

"I'd be happy to show it to you," Josephine said. Taking their drinks with them, Sodipop in tow, the foursome mounted the stairs leading to the third floor. Reaching the lab, Josephine led the way and strode across the room to where the detector was sitting. "This is it," she said. "I named it Lazarus," she added.

Vernon smiled then said "May I look inside?"

"Of course." Josephine opened the detector's door.

Vernon stepped near, bent at the waist and peered inside. "Quite a network of wiring," he said, turning his head this way and that. "What does the final product look like? He straightened and eased back from the detector.

Josephine found the cube in a cabinet, donned surgical gloves and commented   that it was the combination of her mother and father. "The final product." she announced, flourishing the cube between thumb and forefinger.

"Pastor Rainwater said that you caught two 300 pound catfish on that," Vernon said.

"Yes," Josephine said.

"So, you just put some cremated remains in there—Vernon nodded at the detector—and out it came?"

"Actually, there were two of them to begin with. I did some tweaking of the circuitry and the two cubes were joined. I didn't plan it that way, it just happened."

"Quite clever," Vernon said.

"I was just having some fun, keeping bordom at bay, when I discovered that my detector had collected, somehow, a sub-atomic particle mimmicking, I think, the Higgs boson. Though it's only a theory, I think the particle drew the mass of the cremated remains into what you see."

"What prompted you to go fishing with it?" Vernon said, a smile playing at the corners of his mouth.

"Mom and dad loved the lake and fishing. They

wanted to be cremated when they died and mom, especially, wanted their ashes to be cast into the lake. I had this crazy idea—she looked at the detector—of creating something more lasting for them. I really had no idea what would happen."

"And that would be ... "

"It's believed that the cube caused normal sized fish to morph into what Kenny and I brought ashore."

Vernon had become so intrigued by the detector that he seemed to forget the real purpose of his visit which was to persuade Josephine Holland to turn the tide and hopefully put the brakes on the unparalled decline of historically lucrative funeral services before the coffin manufacturers when belly up, taking with them half of the funeral homes in the country. "How large a fish could you catch on that thing?" he said.

"The first fish I caught was a nice one—20 pounds, not unusual in size. I tweaked the power level then Kenny and I went fishing. That's when we caught the two monsters."

"Have you tweaked the machine since?" Vernon asked.

"No, I'm afraid to."

"Why?"

"I don't want to catch a Moby Dick."

Kenny and Streeter laughed. Sodipop barked from beneath a chair in the corner of the room.

Changing the subject somewhat, Vernon said, "Pastor Rainwater said that people thought you accomplished what you did with a common mircowave oven. He said that word has spread that your devise only *looks* like a microwave. But folks are fiddling with theirs anyway, stringing wires, adding buttons and switches, and trying to duplicate what you've done."

"It's crazy," Josephine said. "Even if they succeeded in building what I've built, they don't have the physics equation that's needed to activate. Those are in my head and nowhere else."

"And a lovely head it is?" Vernon said, warming to this remarkably intelligent woman.

"Thank you," Josephine said. Kenny smiled and nodded in agreement.

Jim Streeter of the *Star* had been silent until now. He didn't much care if the coffin industry was saved or not, but he was concerned with the dangerous experimenting that was going on. He had a suggestion: "I could do a story in the *Star* and explain that no amount of experimenting with loved one's cremated ashes in mircowave ovens will produce what Miss Holland has created because she has somehow captured a subatomic particle that appears to be responsible for what has occurred. And she alone possesses the physics equation that will properly activate. I'll predicate the piece by relating what your detector produced and the fish that were caught."

"That might work," Josephine said. "Just don't mention what I think is a particle mimmicking the Higgs boson." And, too, the location of Josephine's home should not be revealed in such a wholesale manner lest she be enundated with visitors. Her cell phone, the only phone she had these days, was not a listed number.

Kenny, who also had been pretty much silent, had a suggestion of his own: "What if you tweaked the detector's energy level, near or at max, and we went fishing again?"

"Another fish fry?" Josephine said.

"Not exactly. Banking on another catch, possibly much larger than before, we could alert food pantries across the Ozarks. Together they could arrange for a refrigerator truck, collect volunteers to help fillet and package the fish, and be on site here."

"Are you *serious*?" Josephine said, her mouth coming ajar.

"Why not? Can you imagine what a nice batch of fresh catfish would mean to a hungry family? It's not something they could afford to buy in a grocery store. If they're on food stamps, I doubt that many of them would want to spend that much of them on something so expensive. Once loaded the truck could park in a more or less central location and the individual pantries could send vehicles and all the ice chests they can muster then return home and give out the fish. They could announce the distribution ahead of time so that folks could be waiting when the fish arrived at their pantry."

"I like it," Jim Streeter said. Vernon Vault agreed. He felt that he had been drawn into something much larger than free falling coffin sales.

"We might be sticking our necks out a mile," Josephine said. "What if a semi pulling a refrigerated trailer shows up and we catch a 20 pound channelcat?"

Everbody laughed. "We roll the dice," Kenny said. "But our two 300 pounders is evidence of what we have done. And if you up the charge on the detector...."

Josephine rubbed her temples, as though she were trying to ease a headache. She gazed at her guests for long moments then said, "Alright, we'll try it. But I don't think Jim should include this in his article in the *Star*. We'll pitch this to the food pantries on our own. If they go for it, well, it'll be time to take mom and dad fishing again." She fell silent and her eyes grew misty.

"What's wrong?" Kenny asked.

"Mom wanted their ashes to be scattered into the lake. This isn't exactly what she had in mind. But I think that a hungry family sitting down to a big plate of fresh catfish would please her and dad very much."

Jim Streeter's piece in *The Kansas City Star* dropped a bombshell on the general public and the world of theoretical physics as well. Though Streeter had not written of the mircowave ovens going ballistic—already rather widely known—the phenomena was creating a firestorm of rumor. Those with a darker turn of mind suggested that maybe Josephine Holland might be a witch and cursing every attempt to duplicate what she had done. One Ozarks man, long steeped in Ozarks lore, thought that an ancient Osage medicine man's spirit was offended and foiling every effort to copycat Josephine's work. This latter notion offered a possible explanation, if only in esoteric terms, though it wouldn't satisfy the most rational minds.

But upon Ellie's next visit to clean, she said that

one of her friends at school, a daughter to the fellow steeped in Ozarks lore, told the class that her dad said mircowaves might be blasting off because the spirit of an Osage medicine man is angry that remains of the dead are "violated" by being put into microwave ovens as though they were nothing more than hot dogs! This sent the class into wild laughter. The inquiring daughter asked her father why Miss Holland's microwave, which really wasn't one, just looked like it, hadn't taken off as so many others had. He said it could be because she had caught heap big fish and fed her neighbors.

The story in the *Star* succeeded in convincing folk—some, at least—that their attempts at doing what Josephine Holland had done were futile and could only end with ruined mircowave ovens and possibly serious injuries or death. And Miss Holland would not assume any liability.

"Interesting, Lt, that you brought an Osage Indian medicine man into this story," Amanda said.

"I couldn't come up with an idea to remotely explain why the microwave ovens were blasting off all over the place. Anyway, if all else fails in rational explanations, hell, bring in the ghosts. They can do anything."

Amanda laughed then said, "Since I wrote the part about the two 300 pound catfish, I've got an idea about what's coming up for the next fishing trip. And I love what you did, Lt, with the food pantry idea. It's so cool! God, I can just *see* people lined up with their ice chests waiting to get some fresh catfish. Can you just imagine the excitement?"

"I can. And I think we may be closing in on a way to end this story, when I don't know."

Chapter Eleven

Kenny and Josephine got on the Internet and found most if not all of the food pantries across the Ozarks. They pitched their proposal to several of them at the outset then asked that each spread the word to their fellow pantries and see what kind of consensus they came up with. Emails began to pour in. All thought it was a wonderful idea. One pantry had a wealthy patron who would arrange for the refrigerated truck. Volunteers for dressing and packaging the fish would be no problem. How many fish? Someone asked. Oh, a regular Moby Dick, Josephine returned in her emails. If this backfires, she had said to Kenny, I may have to leave the state, if not the country.

What might have been a logistical nightmare in arranging for the fish to be dressed and distributed was eclipsed by what to do regarding where to fish for the presumably gigantic catch. Deep water at Palisades where the two 300 pound bluecat were caught was the logical location. But what if the catch—if there was one—were too large to be towed back to Gravois Mills by the pontoon? And what if the nylon line wasn't strong enough? Kenny, being a mechanical engineer, had the answer: "We'll need a truck, 3 ton, perhaps. We'll station it on the opposite shore across from the Palisades bluff then string cable across the lake to where we plan to cast the bait into the water. If we hook something, the truck can head inland and drag our catch to shore where our workers and refrigerated truck will be waiting."

"There's a small sawmill not far from Rainy Creek," Josephine said. "The owner, Slim Pritchard, has a couple of logging trucks. I think he will help us and I'll pay him. But where will we get enough cable to stretch across the lake?"

"The engineering firm I used to work for in Kansas City can manage that," Kenny said. "I'll foot the bill. They might even donate the cable, given the nature of the project. If we haul in something big, it would be great advertising for them."

"And if it's a bust?" Josephine said.

"We'll look into plane tickets for Timbuktu."

Josephine laughed then sobered. "How in the world did we ever get so deep into this?"

"I have no idea. But it's time for a perfect cliché."

"Which one?"

"Too late to turn back now. And I suspect that Jim Streeter's piece in the *Star* has caught the attention of half the wire agencies on the planet."

"Should we tell Streeter what we're about to do now?" Josephine said.

"Might as well. He'll never forgive us if we don't."

"If the *Star* goes to press with this—and they will—we'll have half the state converging on the lake to see what happens," Josephine said.

"We could sell hot dogs and beer."

"Very funny. One other thing," she added. "I think I want my tent back. I can't have it—or, you trampled by hordes that may show up at any time. Which means, of course, with winter not far off, that I think you should move in with me."

"Same bed?" Kenny said with tongue in cheek.

"Possibly. Winters can be awfully cold on the lake.

"Lake-effect?"

"Something like that," Josephine said. "We better give Jim Streeter a call then start arranging for the cable and truck. Do you think we should have something larger than 3 tons?"

"That's a lot of truck; heavy transmission; two speed axle, probably; dual wheels," Kenny said.

"But we'll be using different bait this time," Josephine said.

"How do you mean?"

"Upping the detector's charge joined mom and dad's cube. Lazarus may have supercharged them both."

"Maybe the logging fellow has a 6 ton," Kenny said.

"I'll ask."

Jim Streeter's piece in the *Star* was a proverbial shot heard round the world. He opted, however, upon Kenny and Josephine's advice, not to disclose the exact location of the fishing expedition, hoping that the relative secrecy would stim a tide of an International deluge. Nobody could predict the number of spectators that might show up. Fortunately, though, the northeastern shoreline opposite Palisades bluffs—where the logging truck would be stationed—was without homes for a hundred yards in either direction. The terraine was steep, however; Slim Pritchard's logging truck (he did in fact have a 6 ton GMC for the task) would have its work cut out should something big grab the baited end of the cable.

It wasn't exactly planned as such, but *debarkation* fell on Halloween. Kenny and Josephine considered moving the date on either side of the 31st of October, but too much was in place. "I hope we don't scare the bejesus out of everbody," Josephine said.

Ellie, who was cleaning house this day said, "This is *so cool!*"

The cable—a hundred and fifty yards of it—from Kenny's former employer arrived at the designatied spot. Slim Pritchard, after seeing the great spools of cable and viewing the nearly 45 degree terrain which his old 6 ton workhorse would have to negotiate, tuned the jimmy up: "Runs a little hot sometimes," he said, "smokes a bit, but up to it. She can pull the ass out of a T. rex!"

Late morning on the 31st day of October was when the show would begin, allowing any low fog on the water to rise. It was a crisp morning, though the sky was clear and sun was warming what was believed to be upwards of 5,000 spectators lining the shoreline and pushing up into the timber. A 53' refrigerated semi trailer,

pulled by a bright red Peterbilt tractor had found a relative level patch of ground and sat idling, its diesel engine rattling as though providing a little music for the
occasion. A dozen or more skilled meat cutters sat on
top of the trailer awaiting their cue, should there be one.
Slim Pritchard's GMC was ready and waiting, facing the
lake. The cable was attached to a heavy tow bar on the
front of the truck. "She'll bite better," Slim said, "if we
pull backwards and it'll help keep the front end on the
ground. Otherwise she may rear up if we hook onto
something that you folks think needs this cable." His
left cheek bulged with Red Man chewing tobacco. He
turned his head and spit while eying the cable off the
side of his face.

Kenny, Josephine, Jim Streeter, Ellie and Sodipop
were aboard the pontoon. The end of the cable was
hooked onto the back of the boat. "Let's do it," Kenny
said. Josephine hit the starter and the Merc began to
pure. Murmurs of excitement rolled across the great
crowd. While Josephine set a course for deep water and
the Palisades bluffs a hundred and fifty yards across the
main channel, Kenny opened a storage compartment,
donned the usual surgical gloves for this task and extracted the stainless steel box containing the single cube
that would be attached to the end of the cable when
reaching the wall of the bluff. Sodipop, sitting on Josephine's lap at the boat's controls, barked and switched
his curly cue tail upon seeing the cube come into sight.

Nearing the bluff, Josephine began to idle the Merc
down and eased the boat against the great wall of limestone. There was little wind this day. She used just

enough throttle to keep the boat in position while Kenny prepared the bait. An adjustable ring had been fastened to the end of the cable. Kenny placed the cube within the ring and slowly tightened it just enough to keep it in place. Past experience proved that if something took the bait, the fish would not turn it loose nor would the indestructible cube be damaged.

The bait in place and ready to be thrown overboard, Kenny turned to Josephine and said, "When the bait hits the water, let's get out of here—fast." She nodded and eased the boat away from the bluff just a bit.

"Happy fishing, mom and dad," Josephine said when the bait hit the water with a splash; Kenny scambled to his seat opposite the captain who rapidly pulled away from the bluff and put the Merc's throttle to the gate. Streeter and Ellie sat on a storage compartment and clung to the boat's chrome rail. Ellie had Sodipop in her arms.

More murmurs of excitement rolled across the crowd when seeing the pontoon coming toward them at a high rate of speed. While the boat ran some twenty feet out from the stretched cable, Kenny could see that its weight was taking it to the bottom.

Reaching the opposite shore where all were waiting, Josephine ran the boat ashore 30 yards from the cable then Kenny jumped out and tied the pontoon to a hickory. Josephine cut the engine and took Sodipop into her arms then followed Ellie and Streeter onto the shore and strode to the front of Slim Pritchard's truck. "Any bites yet?" Pritchard said, stuffing a fresh chew into his jaw. He chuckled but sobered quickly when seeing that no one shared his humor.

Thirty minutes passed and the crowd began to grow uneasy, though nobody appeared to be leaving. Slim Pritchard had something of a guarded smirk on his face, glancing fertively at Josephine from time to time. When another thirty minutes had passed, she eased against Kenny and said, "Did you get the cube on good?"

"Yes," Kenny said, not turning to her.

"What's happening?" Ellie said softly.

"Nothing," Josephine replied with a slight edge in her voice. "That's just the problem."

When another half hour passed and some among the crowd began shaking their heads while moving back into the forest and toward where their vehicles were parked, Josephine, looking straight ahead, said to Kenny, "Did you look into tickets for Timbukto?"

"Not yet."

Sodipop growled.

Kenny's words had scarcely left his mouth when the cable sang out like the released bowstrings of a thousand archers sending their arrows into the enemie's battlements. It sent a plume of water fifty feet into the air and for nearly half the distance of the cable's length. A roar swept across the crowd that hadn't begun to leave. Those that had raced back to their spots. Kenny signaled for Pritchard to get his truck running and ready to begin backing up hill. The old GMC was shimmering from the tension put on the cable. Kenny turned to Josephine and said, "Forget Timbukto!"

"My God!" Josephine mumbled. Ellie moved closer to her. Sodipop barked and got against Josephine's leg. She picked him up. Jim Streeter had his note pad out and was writing furiously.

Pritchard fired up the jimmy and it belched a cloud of blue smoke. Kenny motioned for him to start backing slowly. The truck only spun its dual wheels. Pritchard hit the clutch fast and ground the truck's two speed axle into its lowest gear. The truck groaned and shook then began to slowly ease inland. Whatever was caught wasn't giving up without a fight and the truck's flatbed was threatening to come off the ground and losing traction. "We need some weight on the back!" Pritchard yelled. A number of men and boys standing near heard the call for help and began to climb onto the truck's bouncing bed. Others, including women and girls, soon joined them until the truck's wheels began to bite once more as it moved laborously uphill.

The fish had apparently sounded once, but was now relatively near the surface, whiping the cable up and down sending water spray in every direction. "I hope to God the cable holds!" Kenny said.

"Poor mom and dad!" Josephine cried.

Ellie giggled.

Sodipop was whining in Josephine's arms. "Better get the gun," Josephine said, turning to Kenny. He ran to the pontoon and found a .357 that Josephine had bought just in case the .38 wouldn't be adequate. He stuffed a box of cartridges into his pocket.

When he had returned to his place beside Josephine, Pritchard called out of the truck's window, "She's startin' to get hot!"

"Damn!" Kenny mumbled. Steam had not yet begun to boil from beneath the truck's hood. He figured that they hadn't much more time to get the fish to surface and close enough to shoot before the truck gave out. "See if you can get a little more speed out of it!" Kenny called to the driver.

"I'll try!" Pritchard said, grinding gears again and shifting the truck's two-speed axel. It began to move somewhat faster.

Kenny loaded the pistol than turned to Josephine and said, "I don't think that truck can take much more of this. We better get the pontoon out there and hope that the fish surfaces long enough for me to get off a couple of shots."

"Right!" Josephine said. She turned to Ellie and said, "You better stay here, honey, and please hold Sodipop."

"I will," the girl said.

"I'm going with you," Jim Streeter said. Kenny turned to the truck. It was making progress uphill, but steam was beginning to escape from under its hood.

Boarding the pontoon and heading out into the lake, they stayed clear of the thrashing cable though being showered with water. Kenny looked to shore and could see that the smoking truck was giving all it had and was steadily moving inland. He figured that no more than half of the cable had been recovered.

"Kenny!" Josephine yelled. He turned to see water boiling near the surface. Then it appeared with a rush of water that sent a virtual tsunomi to shore where   spectators were scrambling.

"Get in closer!" Kenny called. Josephine nodded, wiping wet hair from her eyes, and brought the pontoon about. Streeter's notpad was soaked and he threw it to the deck and clung to a rail while to boat pitched and rocked.

The creature surfaced just enough for Josephine to identify it, "Flathead!" she cried. The fish was easily twice the length of the pontoon. Kenny spread his legs to steady himself on the boat's wildly rocking deck, held the pistol with both hands and aimed at the monstrous flat head of the fish. He fired off three shots in succession. The bullets went home, sending a spew of blood into the air. Still the fish fought. Kenny aimed and fired three more shots. The fish began to grow still. Kenny looked to shore. Pritchard's jimmy was boiling steam from under its hood but the truck was picking up speed now that the fish had ceased resisting.

Josephine steered the pontoon near the fish while it was being towed to shore. Kenny guessed that it was easily a hundred feet long and could weigh several tons.

The men atop the semi trailer climbed to the ground, opened a compartment under the trailer's belly and pulled out two bundles of tarp. Making their way to where the fish would presumably be bought ashore, they stretched the tarp out then hammered stakes through the metal rings along the tarp's hem to keep it in place when the catch was dragged out of the water and onto the tarp where the cleaning and dressing would take place.

Satisfied that the fish was indeed dead, Kenny and

Josephine broke off and headed for shore where a great many of the crowd were gathering to have a closer look at the fish when it was dragged ashore. Skilled meat cutters talked among themselves regarding their work that would soon be underway. One of the men, an avid fisherman, said that the belly of a flathead catfish is where the best of the meat could be found, though nothing would be wasted. Cameras flashed and videos rolled while Slim Pritchard's steaming truck at last began drawing the fish onto shore and the awaiting tarp. A great cheer and applause erupted across the crowd.

The pontoon had been brought ashore several yards from the fish and the flurry of activity surrounding it. Josephine, Kenny, Jim Streeter and Ellie who still held Sodipop in her arms, sat in curious silence upon the boat. "I want no more of this madness," Josephine said softly, not looking at the others.

"What?" Kenny said.

"No more," Josephine repeated. "It's not natural ... scary as hell." Kenny gazed at her expression that seemed almost cantatonic. Josephine turned to Kenny and said, "Please go get the cube."

Kenny donned surgical gloves as he had done so many times before and soon returned with the cube. "What will you do with this?" he said, holding the cube between thumb and forefinger."

"I don't know," Josephine said. "I've created something that's indestructable it appears. But I'm damn sure done with it. I want my life and privacy back."

"That thing could feed a lot of hungry people," Streeter said, looking at the cube.

"You could sell it," Ellie said.

Josephine cut to Ellie and said, "I've already turned mom and dad into fish bait. *Selling* them would be the last straw."

"How about giving it—them away," Streeter said.

"To whom?"

"Donate—or, loan it to a World Hunger organization," Kenny said.

Josephine's expression began to change as she slowly turned and looked at Kenny.

"Brilliant, absolutely brilliant idea," Streeter said.

"We'll get on the Internet and search world hunger," Kenny said. "We're sure to find an organization that would be interested."

"One other suggestion," Streeter said. "Don't destroy the detector. Just say you did, if you must. Put it under lock and key. For over 50 years most of the world thought that *To Kill a Mockingbird* was Harper Lee's only book. We know better now."

"What's your point?" Josephine said.

"Could you build another detector like the one you have?"

"I doubt it. I was flying by the seat of my pants and simply stumbled onto what I created."

"That's my point," Streeter said. "I once wrote a novel then pitched it. Later I regretted what I had done because, in retrospect, I thought that the story had merit. It had some pretty good scenes. At least it was redeemable. I tried to recreate it but couldn't, not in its original form. The magic had gone back to where it had come from. It wouldn't give me a second chance. You've done something in partical physics that no scientist has ever done. Don't throw it away."

Josephine looked to Kenny and he said, "I think he's right."

"I need to think about this," Josephine said.

"Now what?" Amanda said, while she and Aaron sat beneath a cottonwood and gazed out onto the lake. "I can't just leave my character *thinking* about what to do next."

"I gave her a pretty good idea, I think, about where to go," Aaron said.

"I don't think she wants to invite more attention, International, especially. And I doubt that she can convince the world that she destroyed Lazarus."

"Probably not," Aaron said, "but they'll quit pestering her eventually. I think she's hardheaded enough to stick to her guns. She left the academic world for the sake of a quiet life. She wants it back. The problem, though, is that she's a physicist ... incurable curiosity."

"I'm not following you," Amanda said.

"She's got the equation in her lovely noggin. And I don't see it going away anytime soon."

"I'm getting a sense that *you* don't want it to go away," Amanda said, picking up a stone and giving it a pitch into the lake.

"I think Dr. Holland needs another visitor," Aaron said.

"Like who?" Amanda said, casting a curious look at her partner.

"How about a Nobel Prize physicist, say, from Heidelberg, Germany?"

"Where did you get an idea like that?" Amanda said, sending a flat stone skipping across the water.

"I was offered a scholarship to Heiderberg University once upon a time, before I joined the Marines."

"God! You're so smart, Lt."

"For joining the Marines?"

"You know I love Marines. But Heidelberg University! Why didn't you accept?"

"Cornell has a great literary tradition: E.B. White; James Thurber, to mention only a couple. Though I taught basic physics to high school seniors, my true love is literature."

"Well Mr. Cornell man, let's see what you have in mind for chapter twelve."

Chapter Twelve

Professor Wolfgang von Kepler sat in his favorite chair in the den of his home high on a hill overlooking the campus of Heidelberg University. From the room's large, paned widow he could see the university's towering spires, architecture never to be duplicated in the world in which he now lived.

It was early spring in Heidelberg. Outside his window, Wolfgang could see that the tulips were up, but not yet blooming. He was retired now, Professor Emeritus, and he sometimes longed to be making his way daily across the campus, especially in spring while students, eversoglad to be out of Germany's harsh winter, hurried this way and that on their way to class. He still lectured occasionally on special invitation. Having won a Nobel Prize in physics pretty much assured that he wouldn't be entirely forgotten.

His wife, Anna, had been dead four years now. She chose their home when he was newly ensconced at the university as a young man. She had chosen well, and it comforted him these days, having such a fine view of the campus he dearly loved.

Wolfgang turned from the window when his house-keeper entered the room with coffee and a morning newspaper. Taking up his coffee cup he tested the brew while glancing at the paper before him. He absently set the cup down when noting a story on the front page: Missouri Ozarks Physicist Captures Unknown Particle In Homemade Particle Detector. Wolfgang pushed his coffee from him a bit and drew the paper nearer. The story went on to say that the physicist—Ms. Josephine Holland, not practicing professionally—had been experimenting with creating a new kind of fish bait that would only attract catfish. Just for laughs, and to keep boredom at bay, she put some of her mother and father's cremated remains in the detector—added their DNA, and hit the switch.

Wolfgang chuckled and drew the newspaper a bit closer.

The story continued on the next page and went on to relate how the woman and a mechanical engineer friend brought ashore two 300 pound blue catfish, on the same line, with what the detector created. She later upped the charge on the detector, which she named Lazarus, and in the presence of a great crowd along the shores of Missouri's massive Lake of the Ozarks, and the help of a six-ton logging truck, landed a flathead catfish whose weight could only be guessed at several tons. The meat was to be distributed to food pantries across the Missouri Ozarks.

It's believed, the story continued, that a Higgs boson sub-atomic particle, or one mimmicking the Higgs, found its way into Ms. Holland's detector. *Just for laughs*, it pulled the creamated remains into a mass, two cubes about the size of ice cubes. Then latter, just for laughs, the two cubes were joined as one. Ms. Holland's mother and father had been married for 53 years.

Finishing the story, Wolfgang laid the newspaper aside and took up his coffee cup once more. He thought that he would very much like to talk with Dr. Holland. When his beloved wife was alive they traveled quite a lot during summer recess at the university. They had ventured once to America. He had spent very little of his Nobel Prize money; time to spend some it on another trip to the states, he thought while reaching for his cell phone and connecting with International Information. Ms. Holland's number was unlisted. Probably using a cell phone exclusively as he was these days, he figured. Turning to his laptop computer, Wolfgang searched her name on the Internet. Dr. Josephine Holland, PhDs in molecular biology and particle physics was all that he found. Nothing regarding a physical address, understandably, of course, given privacy issues.

Picking up his laptop Wolfgang rose from his chair and strode across the room to a World Atlas lying open on a table. He turned to the United States and Missouri. All he knew at this point is that Ms. Holland lives somewhere on Lake of the Ozarks, which he found in the central part of the state. Good Lord, he thought while perusing the meadering body of water. Turning to his laptop he searched Lake of the Ozarks and noted that it's considered to be one of the largest man-made lakes in America, if not the world. It has something like

1300 miles of irregular shoreline, more than Lake Michigan or the coast of California. It stretches a 130 miles from one end to the other. Where in God's name should I begin looking for this woman once I get there? Wolfgang wondered. If his plane landed in St. Louis, he would begin his search at the lake's eastern end at Bagnell Dam, he noted. Should he land in Kansas City, his starting point would be at the western end of the lake, near Warsaw, Missouri and Truman Dam.

One thing he didn't want to do, he thought as he more closely inspected the deeply forested geography surrounding the lake, is to search by car on what appeared to be difficult and serpentine county roads. He might never be heard from again. Putting a forefinger to his lips, he looked to the end of the lake nearest St. Louis. Osage Beach, in somewhat bolder letters, might be the best place to start. He searched it on the Internet and found that it hosted several marinas. Perhaps he could charter a boat to take him uplake in search of his prey.

Wolfgang's plane landed in St. Louis at *8:00 a.m* on a Saturday morning. He rented a car and set his sights on Lake of the Ozarks' Osage Beach, easily accessible it appeard from the map of the state he found in the airport terminal. It was a lovely spring morning, much like what he had left in Germany. As he drove Interstate 44 west, the terrain began to grow steeper as he neared the northern edge of the Ozarks plateau. Dogwood were in bloom, though not fully so just yet, as they were in Heidelberg when he left. Not picky about where they call home, Wolfgang thought, observing the trees living happily on the crest of limestone bluffs along the north side of the Interstate as he traveled ever deeper into the central part of the state.

Before leaving home he had done a little research on the state, situated almost exactly in the middle of the country. Heartlanders, some Missourians called themselves. Kansas City is on the 38th parallel. Fertil ground for luminaries of one sort or another: Tennessee Williams, Mark Twain, and Laura Ingalls Wilder in literature; Edwin Hubble of the Hubble Telescope which observed for the first time that everywhere one looked the universe is expanding—at breakneck speed; Harry Truman, of course, who brought the Second World War to a resounding end; Jesse James, not exactly a *luminary*, but famous nonetheless; though bluegrass music isn't what one hears much of in Germany, at least the circles in which Wolfgang traveled, he had read once that Missouri's Rhonda Vincent, unprecedended six consecutive winner of the International Bluegrass Association Female Vocalist of the Year, was to tour parts of Europe; Walt Disney made Missouri his home at the age of 5; and Yogi Berra. The list really does go on and on for this remarkable state, Wolfgang considered when noting his turnoff for heading him more or less directly for Osage Beach.

Wolfgang reached his destination just before noon. The meal during his International flight had been tasty enough, but he was hungry now. It could be said that Osage Beach was Lake of the Ozarks' metropolis, though only a tad over 4,000; boats, boats, and more boats might rival the population, Wolfgang mused when parking his rental in front of the Deep Water Café which advertised a lunch special of fresh catfish, hushpuppies, and sweet iced tea.

Inside the busy café he cast about for a place to sit. Feeling out of place, he considered the one booth that was unoccupied but decided against it, not wanting to take up a whole booth just for himself. Finding a stool at the counter, he wondered if he looked German. There was little doubt when Gladys, a waitress, asked him what he would like and she blinked a couple of times and said, "I'm sorry, sir, I didn't quite get that."

Wolfgang, cognizant of his heavy, German accent, abbreviated his order by simply saying, "Lunch Special."

"Lurch Diesel?" Gladys asked.

"*Lunch Special,*" Wolfgang repeated, with just enough edge to his voice to draw a fleeting glance from a person sitting next to him. *Lurch Diesel* ... for the love of God! Wolfgang whispered. He passed a hand across his brow and smiled at his neighbor, hoping the fellow didn't care to strike up a conversation.

"Coming right up," Gladys said. "I'll bring you your tea."

When Gladys brought him his drink, he wanted to ask her about where the best place might be for chartering a boat, but thought better of it, given the difficulty she had in understanding his order. The café was bustling with business and he doubted that she had time for trying to interpret him. His English was good, gramatically, but Germanic twists on certain words didn't always sit well on American ears, he suspected.

Difficulty in placing his order notwithstanding, Wolfgang found the meal of catfish and hushpuppies very good. The tea was so sweet he wondered if he'd gain a pound or two before exiting the café ... *Lurch Diesel...!* He chuckled all the way to his car.

Wheeling the rental away from the café, he headed for the largest marina in view. Upon reaching it and approaching the first person he saw, he hoped he would have less difficulty expressing his desire to be taxied by boat uplake in search of Dr. Josephine Holland. "I'm in need of someone to take me uplake by boat. I'm looking for someone whose whereabouts I'm unsure of, only that she lives somewhere on the lake," Wolfgang began. "We might have to make a number of stops so that I can go ashore and inquire," he added.

Wolfgang sighed in relief, for the young woman, looking to be in her mid-thirties and quite alert, seemed to be following his request with relative ease. "I can do that," the woman said, glancing at a 19 foot, Chris Craft Mercruiser. A breeze out of the southwest flapped a flag with a martini imprint on the boat's transom.

"How much will it cost?" Wolfgang asked.

"Flat rate of $150, round trip," the young woman said.

That struck Wolfgang as reasonable and he agreed. "When would you like to go?" the young woman said.

"Immediately," Wolfgang said. "I've only to get a couple of bags from my car."

After collecting his bags and being assured that the car would be safe remaining where it sat, Wolfgang went aboard the boat. Its captian, Melisa, he learned after formally introducing himself, turned the key in the boat's ignition and the sterndrive Merc began to purr. "By the way, who are you looking for?" Melisa asked, turning to Wolfgang who had taken a seat across from her where she sat at the boat's helm.

"Dr. Josephine Holland."

Melisa's jaw came slowly ajar. "We'll only have to make one stop, sir. Everybody on this lake knows her and where she lives. Gravois Mills, far end of the lake. It's a ways, but I won't charge you any extra since we won't have to make stops along the way."

"How long will it take?" Wolfgang asked as Melisa backed the boat from the dock.

"Not long. My boat can flat boogie." She eased the boat around in the direction they wanted then slowly pushed the throttle forward. The inboard's 5.7 liter Merc began to whine and the boat quickly reached a plane. Wolfgang looked to the stern where the martini flag was popping in the wind as wake curled away. What a way to travel! he thought, casting a look at his able and lovely captain.

"You flat boogied with that last chapter, Lt," Amanda said.

"Thank you, my dear," Aaron said, stopping on the trail they were taking through the woods. He bowed at the waist. "No encore, just yet. Anyway, I think the two of us will have to work closely together on the next chapter."

"Do you remember the old Laurel and Hardy shows?" Amanda asked when they came to a favorite spring for drinking. A tin cup hung on a tree limb for hikers to use.

"I do," Aaron said, taking the cup and handing it to his partner. "A little before my time, but they turn up on some of the old movies channels."

"Well, this seems like a perfect time to quote Oliver Hardy." Amanda finished a drink of water, handed the cup to Aaron then said, quoting Hardy, "Here's another fine mess you got me into."

Finishing his own drink from the spring, Aaron hung the cup back on the tree, wiped his mouth on the sleeve of his tee shirt then said, "We may have bitten off more than we can chew."

"So...."

"We chew it," Aaron said, taking Amanda's hand and continuing along the trail.

Chapter Thirteen

"Gravois Mills up ahead," Melisa said, pointing toward the northeastern shoreline. Wolfgang craned his neck to have a better look at his destination.

"I guess we'll have to ask around to find out which place belongs to Dr. Holland," Wolfgang said above the hum of the boat's engine.

"No need," Melisa said, beginning to ease the boat's throttle back. "That's her place there, the three-storied log house. "She has a big fish fry each summer, everybody invited. I never miss it."

Melisa skillfully navigated the boat alongside Josephine Holland's dock, opposite her pontoon. She asked Wolfgang to disembark and secure a line which he did. "Ms. Holland isn't expecting me," Wolfgang said. "I'm not entirely sure that I'll be welcome or how long I'll be. Would you mind waiting here with my bags until I find out?"

"No problem," Melisa said, cutting the boat's engine.

Wolfgang drew a deep breath and released it slowly

as he made his way off the dock and toward the house. He heard a small dog bark. A woman with a remarkable head of strawberry blonde hair came out onto the home's deck. A man soon joined her. She put a hand above her eyes to shield the sun's glare coming off the water. Reaching a short flight of stairs that led to the deck, Wolfgang said, "Good morning."

"Good morning to you, sir," Josephine said. Sodipop was at her side and he barked once and switched his curly cue tail in greeting the visitor. Ellie was present this day and she soon appeared on the deck.

"Forgive me for just dropping in on you unannounced," Wolfgang said, slightly out of breath. Josephine smiled and gazed curiously at the old gentleman whose hair was white as a dogwood blossom. Wolfgang extended a hand and introduced himself, "I'm Wolfgang von Kepler."

Josephine blinked once and her chin rose a bit. "Dr. Wolfgang von Kepler of Heidelberg University?"

"Yes."

Josephine and Kenny introduced themselves and Ellie, Sodipop as well. Wolfgang reached and stroked the dog's head.

"And to what do I owe the pleasure of meeting a Noble Prize winner?" Josephine said.

"I saw a story in our Heidelberg newspaper a few days ago and I decided that I must meet you, my dear. My plane landed in St. Louis and I rented a car and drove to Osage Beach where I chartered a boat to bring me here." He glanced back at the Chris Craft resting alongside the dock. Josephine beckoned to the boat's captain to come and join them on the deck.

When Melisa had joined them, Josephine suggested that they go inside. They weren't long into their conversation when Josephine insisted on Wolfgang spending a few days as her and Kenny's guest, if he hadn't any pressing plans. He said that he didn't and had, infact, brought along a couple of bags. He chuckled at what might appear to be presumption on his part. Josephine fixed lunch. Afterward, Wolfgang and Melisa excused themselves and went out onto the deck where Wolfgang paid for the boat's services. He asked if Melisa might come for him when he was ready. She agreed and gave Wolfgang her cell phone number.

It was late afternoon and Josephine suggested that they have cocktails and sit on the deck. Wolfgang quickly directed the conversation toward the real purpose of his visit. "What you have done, Ms. Holland with your homemade detector has rocked the world of particle physics to its very foundation. I'm surprised that you've not been absolutely enundated with scientists and reporters."

"I'm not easy to find," Josephine said. "I've had some visits, though, but none of your stature, Dr. von Kepler. I'm afraid I've been rude to some of them. Anyway, it must have worked. I've been pretty much left alone."

"Until now," Wolfgang said, smiling.

"I welcome your visit. May I call you Wolfgang?"

"Please do. Of course I'm very much interested in having a look at your detector. And if the mysterious particle suspected of being a Higgs boson, or one that is mimmicking it as the newspaper story related, is something I can have a look at, I would find that most intriguing. I'm not here to spy on you, my dear, and I'll not ask to see any equations that you've entered."

"I would have no problem sharing the equations with you, Wolfgang," Josephine said. "Without my detector, it would not be possible to duplicate what I've done."

"Most wise of you to take such safety measures," Wolfgang said. "By the way, have you gone fishing again?"

Kenny laughed softly and turned his attention to Josephine. "I haven't. And I don't know that I ever will again."

"Why not?" Wolfgang said, sampling his drink.

"It's freaky, downright scary. I should never have messed around with something like that."

"Do you still have the cube?" Wolfgang asked.

"I do."

"Of course I'd very much like to see the detector," Wolfgang said.

"Let's take our drinks and go to my lab now," Josephine said.

Sodipop, having learned the word *lab* long ago, led the way and headed for the stairs.

"Smart dog," Wolfgang said, falling in behind Josephine.

Reaching the lab, Josephine stepped aside and let Wolfgang enter first. Sodipop hopped onto a favorite chair under which he sometimes hid when things in the lab got a little too scary for his liking. Wolfgang gazed about at the spacious room and up at the skylight. "Marvelous place to work," Wolfgang said.

Josephine swept one hand toward the detector and said, "There it is." Wolfgang strode to the machine and peered through the glass. Josephine turned on her computer then entered the code for unlocking the machine's door. She opened it and Wolfgang moved near and looked inside. "My goodness, what interesting circuitry..." Looking all about inside the detector he said, "Where is the cube that half the world is talking about?"

"I keep it locked away," Josephine said. She strode to a cabinet and extracted the stainless steel box containing the cube. She opened the box then handed Wolfgang a pair of surgical gloves. "You may touch it if you like," she said.

Gently touching the cube with his right hand, he said, "It's rather warm. Have you checked for radio activity?"

"We did, some time back," Kenny put in.

Josephine sensed that Wolfgang would like some sort of demonstration, short of another fishing trip. She donned a pair of gloves and put the cube in the detector, locked the door and began entering code.

"You have physics software I assume," Wolfgang said while Josephine typed. She nodded.

Josephine typed and the request crawled across the 42 inch screen: Identify composition of cube.

Wolfgang smiled and glanced at Kenny.

Composition cannot be indentified ... has undegone cloaking technology not accounted for....

"It's since been discovered, as you no doubt know,"

she added, turning to Wolfgang. "But only I have the equation for activating."

"Which is to say nobody can duplicate what you've done," Wolfgang said.

"Exactly."

"Would you mind letting me see the mysterious particle?" Wolfgang said.

Josephine began typing equation that would bring up the particle. Wolfgang blinked a couple of times at the speed at which the symbols were racing across the screen. He was able to decipher and he drew a deep breath and released it slowly.

The screen darkened then a light began coming forward slowly, as if traveling from deep space. The screen settled into a steady, rather charcoal tone. In the center of the screen was a tiny speck. Josephine began typing again and the speck grew larger until it appeared as a small disk. It had no spin and sat quite still with the exception of a slight rocking motion. "That's the little gizmo," Josephine said.

Kenny laughed softly.

Josephine looked to Wolfgang. His face had blanched. Then a faint smile began to animate his face. "Dr. Kepler," she asked. "Sir..." she said, looking more directly into his face.

"I, uh, yes," he said, seeming to come to his senses. "May I use your computer?" he asked

"Certainly."

Wolfgang took a seat at the computer and began typing. Josephine felt the fine hair on the back of her neck beginning to tingle. She looked to Sodipop and he had gotten under the chair. Nobel Prize winner Wolfgang von Kepler is in my lab, typing on my computer, Josephine thought while her breath came a little short. Equations that she had never seen before were racing across the screen. My God! What is he doing? she thought, shooting a look at Kenny.

Wolfgang quit typing abruptly. He stared at the particle on the screen. It stopped rocking then did what looked like a backflip. "Well, well, well, who do we have here?" Wolfgang said.

Josephine's mouth was coming ajar as she moved closer to the screen. "What's been mimicking the Higgs boson my dear isn't a subatomic particle at all"

"What are you saying?" Josephine said, moving closer to the screen.

"Benign Poltergeist," for lack of a better term, Wolfgang said, not taking his eyes off the screen.

"Jeeesus," Kenny mumbled.

"What …how…?" Josephine asked, completely lost for words.

Wolfgang was quite calm when he turned to Josephine. "Before I left Heidelberg I did some interesting research into your state of Missouri. You folks have produced an amazing number of celebrities and luminaries. I think that it has something to do with your state riding so close to the 38th parallel which is serving as an extraordinary nexus in which certain, high intensity forces travel."

"I don't believe in spirits, Poltergeists, and things like that," Josephine said.

With that, Wolfgang turned to the computer once

more and began to type: Identify yourself, please. He turned to Josephine and Kenny and said just above a whisper, "Always say please to a Poltergiest, even the good ones."

Good afternoon, Dr. Kepler. We meet again, came words across the screen.

We do indeed, Wolfgang typed.

Sodipop growled from beneath the chair. Josephine took Kenny's hand.

Well, you've caused something of a stir in this lovely woman's life, Wolfgang typed.

If I've caused her any anguish, I'm so sorry. It's just that I've been up and down, up and down, back and forth back and forth in this nexus and I've had no fun for the longest time! When I came across this dear woman and saw the toy she had built, I thought this would be my chance to have some real excitement.

"Does he—it—whatever have a name?" Josephine said.

"Possibly, but it's never been divulged, to my knowledge," Wolfgang said.

"Does it have a computer to type on?" Ellie asked.

"No," Wolfgang said, "it simply *thinks* it's response onto the screen."

"Ask how Poltergiest has turned up in my house?" Josephine said. Wolfgang typed the question and Poltergiest responded:

Dr. Holland entered an equation—inadvertently, perhaps, that opened a port in the nexus. That's how I discovered her.

"Ask if concealing the cube's compositon was Poltergiest's doing," Josephine said.

Wolfgang typed the question to Poltergeist:

Yes. I've sensed for some time Miss Holland's reluctance to let the cube's compostion be known. So I helped her out. She has, of course, let the compostion be known of late. But what she has done cannot be duplicated without the activating equation in her head which I have not been able to infiltrate. Even if I could I wouldn't betray her wishes. What she has done is truly remarkable. I've simply chosen to compliment her work a bit.

Most kind of you, Wolfgang typed.

Thank you.

"How did you suspect something like this?" Josephine said to Wolfgang.

"I've had some experiences," Wolfgang said. "And that's all I'll say. Being caught red-handed fiddling in things esoteric would be most scandelous for a Nobel Laureate."

"How do we know that this is a Poltergeist?" Kenny said. Josephine nodded in agreement.

Wolfgang began typing: We have a couple of skeptics in the room. They need proof.

As you know, Dr. Kepler, I'm not your average Poltergeist. I was pretty much kicked out of Poltergeistdom for refusing to continue turning over tables, chairs, slaming doors, screeching and howling and scaring the everlasting crap out of perfectly nice people.

Just do something mild, Wolfgang typed.

Very Well.

With that the chair under which Sodipop was hid-ing began to rise and it rose all the way to the ceiling and began to rotate. Sodipop watched it for a moment then bolted for the stairs.

Wolfgang chuckled then typed: That will do, I think. He looked to Josephine and Kenny while they watched the chair easing its way back to the floor.

"Ask Mr. Poltergeist if he was responsible for the microwaves going ballistic."

Wolgang typed her question.

That was Sleeping Bear's doing, the old Osage medicine man. I tried to dissuade him but he wouldn't listen. He was so angry that he threw his peace pipe into the lake.

"Tell Mr. Poltergeist that I want nothing more to do with the cube, but it appears to be indestructable," Josephine said.

Wolfgang held Josephine's gaze for long moments then began typing: Dr. Holland wants nothing more to do with the cube but has found it to be indestructable. Long moments passed and Wolfgang was about to begin typing again to restate the desire when Poltergeist responded.

Is Dr. Holland quite sure?

Josephine nodded in the affirmative.

Yes, she's quite sure, Wolfgang typed.

It seems such a shame, Poltergeist said. *But I can dispose of it for her.*

"How?" Josephine said to Wolfgang who typed the question

I'll see to it.

"That's not a very good answer," Josephine said to Wolfgang.

"We'd better leave well enough alone," Wolfgang said

Please put cube in Detector and activate. No further equation will be needed, said Poltergeist.

Josephine fetched the cube and held it for a few moments then said, "Goodbye, mom and dad. It was fun—sort of." She gently placed the cube in the detector and hit the start button.

The detector began to hum. It glowed green, then purple, red, back to green then grew dark and shut down. Sodipop had returned to the top of the stairs but didn't enter the room, only sticking his head around the corner.

Josephine unlocked the detector's door. She started to open it but hesitated. She turned to Kenny and said, "Please open the door."

Kenny did as she wished. The detector was empty.

Wolfgang typed: The deed is done.

Yes, the deed is done.

"Ask if Mr. Poltergeist is to be a permanent neighbor," Josephine said.

Wolfgang typed her question.

No. I'm leaving your country. I have business elsewhere, one could say.

Wolfgang spent two days in Josephine's home, at the end of which he called Melisa and asked that she pick him up at her convenience. He would take a plane later in the day for Heidelberg. During the boat ride back to Osage Beach and his car, he wondered if Josephine had been wise to trust a Poltergeist, albeit a presumably harmless one. Oh well, he thought, *the deed is done.*

Two Weeks Later

It was Friday evening and Ellie had come later in the day to clean. She finished a little after 5:00. During supper, Josephine talked of how glad she was to be done with the whole thing regarding the cube.

Regarding the Poltergeist, Wolfgang said that his lips were sealed. Good thing, Josephine said. She was the butt of this joke, and if it got out, she would be the laughing stock of the entire scientific community, albeit beloved by mediums the world over. Jim Streeter might very well be fired from *The Kansas City Star* for being so duped. As for Dr. Porter, she had been duped as well, but found the whole thing quite amusing. Josephine wondered at times if she herself might have to move to Timbuktu afterall, even considered smashing Lazarus to smithereenes, but Kenny convinced her otherwise. She locked it away in a closet. Out of sight but not out of mind.

Ellie joined them for supper. Sodipop was having a bowl of dog chow. At 5:30 Josephine rose and turned on the T.V. for the evening news. The familiar face and voice of the anchorman came on. "We have a most unusual story coming to you tonight somewhere off the coast of Africa," he began. "A saltwater catfish of unbelievable size has been caught and brought ashore."

The image of the fish and huge crowd surrounding it came onto the screen. The fish looked to be nearly 3 stories high and great ladders had been laid against it where workers were busy dressing the fish and throwing large slabs of the meat down to workers below. There was singing and dancing in the background and fires were burning in both directions along the beach as far as the eye could see where fish was being boiled, fried, roasted, and sometimes cleaverly seasoned with herbs and spices.

"Details are still coming in regarding how this fish was caught," said the anchorman. "Early reports say that no hooks or gaffs were used. One bystander who wished to remain anonymous said that he saw someone remove something that was fastened on the end of a cable that brought the fish ashore then disappear into the crowd. The fish was landed with the help of a D7 Caterpillar."

"Please fix me a drink, Kenny," Josephine said in a voice so low it was barely heard.

"I'll have one too," Kenny said, rising but not taking his eyes off the T.V.

"My grandma believed in ghosts," Ellie said, taking a fork to her blackberry cobbler "She said you should never believe a Poltergeist, no matter what they say."

Sodipop finished his food and came to Ellie. She took him onto her lap.

Kenny returned from the wet bar and handed Josephine her drink. He sat down beside her. He glanced at her but said nothing. She was shaking her head slowly from side to side in disbelief. She swept tears from her cheeks upon seeing a woman hand feeding freshly baked fish to a small child with distended stomach and large eyes. "I wish mom and dad could see this," Josephine said in a voice that broke with rising emotion.

"Maybe they can," Ellie said, snuffing at her own tears. Sodipop switched his curly cue tail and barked, just once.

"We did it, Lt," Amanda said, snuggling next to Aaron when he turned out the lantern in their tent.

"We did, girl. We'll need to do some fine tuning, you know, clean up a thing or two. It was only the first draft."

"Do you think we can sell it to a publisher?"

"We can try. We better type it, though. I've got a laptop in my Suburban ... haven't had a need for it out here. It's got a good battery. We can recharge with power converter in Suburban. We'll take the file into Camdenton and print copies and start sending them to agents. I've got a mailbox on a post up at the road."

Three Months Later

Amanda and Aaron sat by their campfire. Aaron was roasting turkey dogs. Amanda was counting rejection slips. "How many?" Aaron said.

"Thirty," Amanda said.

"Let's not send the manuscript out anymore for a while," Aaron said. "This is brutal."

"Yes it is," Amanda said, pitching the papers into the fire.

The call came in on Aaron's cell phone during the early afternoon on a beautiful fall day. "Hello," Aaron said, noting the out-of-state area code and glancing at Amanda.

"Aaron?"

"Yes."

"This is Cynthia Jones calling from Burbank, California."

"Yes, Miss Jones."

"I received your manuscript. I have bad news and good news."

"Agent from California," Aaron mouthed to Amanda whose mouth flew wide.

"I haven't had any luck selling the story to a publisher."

"Oh," Aaron said, casting a downcast glance at Amanda.

"The good news is that I've found a filmmaker who loves the story and wants to buy its film rights."

"Filmmaker," Aaron mouthed. Amanda clapped her hands and fell backward, bycycling her feet in the air.

"Would this be agreeable to you and Amanda?"

"Uh, yes," Aaron said, clearing his throat.

"I'll send you a contract. If it meets your approval—the two of you—then sign and return as soon as possible."

"How much will we get?" Amanda whispered.

"What, uh, do you think we will get?" Aaron said.

"I'll get the best deal I can without scaring the man off. But given the filmmaker's excitement—inspite of you and Amanda being unknown—I think it's safe to say you two will no longer need to live in a tent. Something else, too, I should mention. If the film is decently successful, a book deal might follow. That's kind of backward, but it's sometimes done."

"Where would the movie be made?" Aaron asked

"On site, no doubt," on your Lake of the Ozarks."

"Will we be allowed to watch?" Aaron said.

"Certainly, and I'm sure the director will want some input from the two of you since you wrote the story."

When the conversation ended, Aaron and Amanda rolled about in each other's arms and laughed like children. "Oh God, Lt! We'll be so rich and famous!"

The production of their book hit the big screen for the holidays the next year. It didn't break any box office records; it was one of those sleepers, critics said. And though reviews weren't rave, they were decent. The most savvy of reviewers thought the film had been cheated by the screenplay being *based*—rather loosely—on the story and not adapted which would have followed the original story more closely. Leading into Oscar night the film had gotten no nominations. That disappointment faded quickly when the book's publishing rights were bought and a beautifully designed hardcover kicked butt all the way to the top of the New York Times and slammed the door behind it for 16 weeks.

One Year Later

Amanda opened the screened door and came onto the

home's expansive front deck. She had a baby in each arm while she carefully carried a glass of iced tea. She set the tea down on a table then handed the babies— twins, boy and a girl—to her husband. "Lt, please hold them for a moment while I bring your tea," she said. Coming back onto the porch, she took one of the babies then sat down in a cane chair and bared a breast to nurse. She sipped her tea and gazed at her husband. "You're just the best daddy, Lt."

"Thanks.

"I was at Pine Cove Store yesterday and I met two ladies who can come and help with the reunion. Having both of our families here will be a houseful. The ladies said they would be happy to help with anything, cook- ing, cleaning whatever."

"Sounds like a good idea to me," Aaron said, kissing the head of the baby girl in his arms. "We'll have a houseful, alright" he added, "plenty of room, though, three stories and all. You designed it just like Jose- phine's. Her lab is our sunroom, of course."

"It'll be one of the proudest days of my life when mom and dad and my sisters see it and our twins. They don't think I'm such a looser anymore. Mom said she bought 10 copies of our book and gave them to friends. The movie is coming out in DVD soon. She's buying several of those too."

Amanda finished breast feeding the baby boy, put a dish towel over her shoulder and burped him. She ex- changed babies with Aaron then bared her other breast for the girl. "Did I ever thank you for taking me in, Lt?" she said.

"Probably."

"Well, in case I didn't—thanks. I never thought I'd have a husband like you and a wonderful house like this, and built right where your tent was when I met you. Was I scary that night with my wet hair down in my face?"

"I thought you were a ghost from the graveyard," Aaron said.

Amanda laughed then said, where's Sodipop?"

"Out there," Aaron said, pointing to where the dog was lying in the shade of a willow, looking out onto the lake and watching the boats. Upon hearing her name, the Havanese turned and looked toward the house. She barked once and switched her curly cue tail.

"Did she get her saucer of Mountain Dew?" Amanda said, shifting a bit in her chair to accommodate the nursing baby.

"Yeah. I think we need to put her on the diet version, though. She's gaining some weight."

CPSIA information can be obtained
at www.ICGtesting.com
Printed in the USA
LVOW03s1926161017
552622LV00001B/57/P